SPIRIT OF A HERO

EDDIE ROY

SPIRIT OF A HERO

EDDIE ROY

CHAPTER 1

"Please God,
Not Another One"

At three a.m. Thursday morning, the eighteenth of May 2022, the Chief of Police of Martin's Grove, New Mexico groped in the dark for the bedside stand and slapped his hand down on the receiver of the blaring phone that was wedged between the lamp and his coffee thermos. Grabbing the receiver and jamming it to his ear he shouted, "Smythe-Bates here." Even with his sleep muddled voice, the Scottish/British accent was unmistakable. Sounding confused, the man on the other end said, "Chief?"

Tired and impatient, Smythe-Bates said, "Mr. Johnson, who else in this God-forsaken town would answer the phone Smythe-Bates?"

"Johnson?" Officer Johnson mumbled, "Right, Chief. I just can't get used to the way you answer."

"Well how did your last chief answer his phone?"

Johnson mumbled: "He said hello."

"So, what is it, Johnson?" The chief asked. Then he added, "It better be important!" The officer hesitated, and then replied, "I'm sorry chief, but it is important, real important. I am awful sorry; this is bad, and it's really damned important." Officer Johnson's voice hitched a little and the Chief felt certain he heard the man sniffing back some tears.

And just that quickly, the Chief knew what this was about and said, "Please, dear God, not another one." Once again Officer Johnson's voice hitched and he was now audibly sobbing, almost unable to continue the call. But he pulled himself together and said: "Yeah Chief, another one. That makes four now, four out of the five. I'm sorry as hell but this time they lost one of their residents."

The fire suppression system was activated but the fire was set in the kitchen, just like the others." Johnson paused, then went on, "Only this time, the wing of the building where the kitchen was located also had five resident's rooms. It was an old place; it wouldn't pass code now, they'd never build it that way today."

"I'm well aware of how many this makes, but this time someone died?" the Chief asked.

"Yes. An 80-year old man named Pete Casper. He resided in the room adjacent to the kitchen and store-room. By the time the fire department arrived, it was too late. The poor old gentleman was gone. The EMT said he died from smoke inhalation, at least he didn't burn." Johnson fell silent.

Smythe-Bates said, "That's little consolation to Mister Casper." Then the Police Chief asked:

"Where was it?"

"It was Golden Years Elder Care out on Airfield Road north of town." "I know where it is, it's on the map," the Chief said. He'd had a large map of the town and the surrounding areas tacked to the wall of his office since the day he'd taken over the space. Every nursing home in or around the town was marked by a red flag with the facility's name attached. "Okay Johnson, I'll meet you there in twenty minutes. Contact Leonard Dunn and ask him to meet us there, unless he's already there. I don't know if the Fire Chief goes out on every call"

"Will do Chief…and Chief, I'm sorry about not recognizing your voice. It'll take me a while. No matter what I hear you say, you always sound like Sean Connery to me."

"That's all right. There are a lot worse people I could sound like than Sean Connery. You've always sound like Sam Elliot to me." Johnson snickered:

"There are worse people I could sound like too."

The Chief said: "Right, see you in twenty." The men disconnected.

A half-hour later dozens of people were milling around the smoking pile of rubble that had until recently been the Golden Years Elder Care nursing home, one- half-mile from town on Airfield Road. The road's name hadn't changed although the air field had been shut down for twenty years. The running joke was that neither the county nor city could afford a new road sign. Police Chief Smythe-Bates and Fire Chief Leonard Dunn stood off to themselves discussing the situation in private. Looking at the smoldering remains of the building, Dunn shook his head and said, "Why in the hell would someone torch four nursing homes?"

"I have no idea, but that's what I was hired to figure out. So far, I haven't done a very good job of it. I need to solve this before he goes after the remaining one."

"Well, the first two didn't happen on your watch," Dunn pointed out. The last Chief didn't have a clue how to even begin to investigate the case. That's why he's not Chief anymore. They damned near ran him out of town on a rail."

"Well, on my watch or not, there had to be clues left behind and my job is to find and follow them. No one died in the first two fires so now we're not just after a serial arsonist, but a serial arsonist who also happens to be a murderer."

The Fire Chief said: "I sure don't envy the task you've taken on. You put yourself in one a hell of a position here and I can't for the life of me understand why you pulled up stakes and left London for this little one-horse-town." The Police Chief said: "You were at my interview; did you sleep through it? I thought I made myself exceptionally clear."

The Fire Chief replied: "No, I was wide awake. If you'll remember, I asked you the same question then and if I hadn't, the mayor or somebody else on the city council would have."

"Actually, the mayor asked me that exact question on the telephone the first time we spoke. It was just after I'd contacted him to say I was interested in the job as your Police Chief.

CHAPTER 2

20 Days Earlier - Interview Meeting

Mayor Poole sat in the center on one side of a sixteen-foot-long table in the plain but adequate meeting room on the old adobe city hall's second floor. Eight folding chairs were lined up on either side of him. Those chairs held the members of the city council, the town's fire chief and members of the small police force and fire department. Also in attendance were some of the town's leading citizens, business owners, school principals, civic leaders, and the like. On the other side of the table was just one chair directly across from Mayor Poole. It was currently empty.

When a rap came at the hall door the mayor looked at the wall clock and said, "That's a good sign already, exactly four o'clock. Promptness is a good virtue…time to begin." He went to the door, opened it, and shook hands with the man who entered. After seating him across from his own chair, the mayor made obligatory introductions and called the meeting to order. The only name that had stayed with the new participant was that of Leonard Dunn, the Fire Chief. Because of the circumstances that had drawn him to this town, the Fire Chief sat to the mayor's immediate left.

The mayor made a production of straightening a stack of papers before him on the table. Then he said, "Ladies and gentlemen, everyone knows why we're here. Inspector Smythe-Bates has come all the way from London to discuss the possibility of becoming our new Chief of Police."

"Mister," the guest of honor said. Surprised and confused, the mayor queried: "I'm sorry?" "It's Mister; I haven't been an Inspector for nearly a year."

"Oh, right, sorry," Mayor Poole said as his face turned just slightly red. Then anxious to get back on track he glanced to his left and right and said, "I must say I have an advantage over the rest of you.

I've had a chance to do some study of Mr. Smythe-Bates' background and qualifications. Let's start off by seeing if any of you have questions for him."

From both sides of the Mayor, hands shot up like a group of high school seniors competing for a full-ride college scholarship. The Mayor chuckled and said: "If it's okay with you Mr. Smythe-Bates, I'll just do a brief run-down of the pertinent information I have on hand. It might help answer a lot of the questions that would undoubtably come up and save us some time. Smythe-Bates nodded and politely said: "That's fine with me." The mayor looked at the top sheet of a multi-page print-out and began reading:

Edwin Smythe-Bates served as a deck officer for five years in Her Majesty's Naval Service before a twenty-year career as an Inspector-Detective first-class with Scotland Yard, now retired. During his years of service with Scotland Yard he was awarded virtually every commendation obtainable for exceptional service and outstanding performance.

The Fire Chief interjected, "It was you!" His interruption earned him a scorn from the mayor that truly would have killed him if looks could actually do so. "Still," the Fire Chief continued:

You caught the Soho Torcher." Smythe-Bates shifted in his chair and said: "You're familiar with that case?"

"Every firefighter in the world has heard about

that case!" the Fire Chief yelled. Then he turned to the mayor and said: "You've got to hire this man. If you don't hire him now, you're the biggest fool who ever walked on two legs."

The mayor's face turned a beet-red and a low growling sound actually emanated from his throat. Finally, after drawing a few deep breaths, he got himself somewhat under control and irritably asked of the room in general:

"All right, who the hell is the Soho Torcher?" Smythe-Bates answered: "Eight years ago, a serial arsonist was burning London hotels." Once again, the fire chief interrupted:

"Seven of them, wasn't it?" The mayor said, "For God's sake Leonard, let the man talk."

"Yes sir." Smythe-Bates continued: "The first three were in the Soho district; that's how he got that ridiculous name. The press did that, not us. Then he moved on to other areas, but always utilizing the same methods. He was quite amateurish but very effective. All of the hotels were owned by the same man. Naturally, popular belief immediately hypothesized he was burning them for the insurance money. But I opined that the theory just made zero sense."

"'How so?" Mayor Poole asked."

"The man was an enormously wealthy real estate tycoon but the hotels weren't considered high-end establishments. The combined insurance payoffs on the all hotels were significantly less than the total value of his exotic auto collection; he simply didn't need the money." So, who did it turn out to be and how did you figure it out?" Mayor Poole queried.

Smythe-Bates smiled and said : "Simple deduction and a life-long fascination with the Bard." The fire chief said, "What in the hell is the Bard?" A stern-looking red-headed woman sitting beside him delivered the sort of elbow to the ribs that could only be delivered by a wife, and whispered loudly in his ear, "Shakespeare, you idiot." The fire chief nodded toward the redhead and said, "My wife and keeper, Monica."

Without waiting to be asked, Smythe-Bates explained: "After a careful review, I deduced it closely resembled a Romeo and Juliet scenario. The daughter of the hotel owner was infatuated with a young bar musician and her father deemed that minstrel not worthy of her. He and his family were clearly not up to the father's standards. In fact, at one point the old man had the boy beaten to a bloody pulp to dissuade him from seeing her. Rather than commit suicide or give up and run away, this "Romeo" chose revenge and proceeded to burn the father's hotels."

"And you figured that out," Mayor Poole asked, rather amazed. Former Inspector-Detective Smythe-Bates nodded: "Indeed I did." The mayor said:

"Mr. Smythe-Bates, I have only one question, if you don't mind."

"Not at all.

Please, ask away." I can't help but wonder. A man who is so clearly over-qualified for this job could've easily picked from hundreds of positions, either in America or the UK. Why are you willing to leave your home and over 5,000 miles to a little town in the middle of nowhere? Forgive me or being blunt, but you can't need a job in Martin's Grove that much."

Smythe-Bates stood up, put his hands in his hip pockets, cleared his throat and said: " Mayor Poole, a little over a week ago I came down to breakfast and my wife Kathrine had opened The New York Times, which she reads regularly, and showed me the story of what's been happening here in your fair hamlet. I read it carefully and then she and I had a serious conversation. Then I contacted you and following our long chat, we set up this meeting. Kathrine and I flew into Santa Fe and rented a car yesterday morning. She's waiting at the hotel now to see what news I bring. Once our meeting here is over, she and I will decide how to proceed.

So, Mister Mayor and the rest of you fine folks, I'm not here because I need a job. I'm here because you and your town need help. Also, my wife has always been fascinated with American western movies and television shows. When she recalled that The Rifleman television series was set in New Mexico, it was another selling point on the whole idea. She knew the town of North Fork was fictional but she still wanted to see the western United States. And like they say: Happy-Wife, Happy Life." The Fire

Chief rolled his eyes at the redhead beside him and mumbled, "They say that, do they?"

Smythe-Bates said: "Mayor Poole, I have a question for you, if you don't mind."

"What's that?" said the Mayor, with one eyebrow cocked. "How can a town with a population of less than seventeen-thousand need *or* support five elderly care homes?"

"We had a mayor back in the nineteen sixties to thank for that, he was quite a businessman. He'd heard that doctors back east were telling their patients about the benefits of a dry, arid climate in the Southwest. He began promoting the idea through mailings and various promotional materials to fellow physicians and medical facilities and mentioned our area as a suitable location. He was careful to do nothing illegal. He went as far as advertising in national magazines and medical journals. Before long he started getting some inquiries. Slowly, a few people with ailments moved here, looking for those miracle cures. Some got worse, gave up and moved away.

But when a few improved, whether it was because of our miracle air, or the prescriptions they would be taking anyway, then they couldn't wait to give sworn testimonials.

More and more people moved here…a lot more. Soon the town grew by leaps and bounds. When a town has more citizens, it eventually has citizens growing old," the mayor finished with a flourish.

"Thank you, Mr. Mayor, that explains a lot." Acknowledged Smythe-Bates.

With a slight bow Mayor Poole said:

"I make a motion that we officially offer the position of Chief of Police of Martin's Grove to Edwin Smythe-Bates." Hands shot up throughout the room and a chorus of 'second the motions' sounded out like a choir trying in vain for harmony.

Then the mayor said:

"The last order of business before we officially adjourn is to recognize Pastor Windor from the First Lutheran Church."

A young man wearing sweat pants and a baggy t-shirt with a cross emblazoned on the front stood up and said:

"Chief Smythe-Bates, our church owns a house that was formerly used as a parsonage but now stands empty. You and your wife are welcome to use it as long as you need. Also, welcome to our town. We're located on Second Street with services every Sunday at 10:00 A.M., please feel free to join us."

CHAPTER 3

Small Clues

The two chiefs, Police Chief Smythe-Bates and Fire Chief Dunn met at the scene of the most recent nursing home fire. Chief Dunn pulled into the parking lot and got out of his SUV wearing a black Stetson cowboy hat with a rattlesnake-skin band. Smythe-Bates pointed at it and said: "You weren't wearing that at the interview." Dunn replied: "I was when I got there but my wife made me take it off. I guess she thought it wouldn't make a good first impression." The new Chief said: "That's a damned shame, because I like it. Where might I get one?"

"In New Mexico? You can get a cowboy hat at just about any store. Walmart has a big selection, and you can get them in most convenience stores or gas stations."

Smythe-Bates said: "America is going to take some getting used to, now let's get this over with."

"Okay" Replied Chief Dunn.

All that remained of the Golden Years Elder Care building was a huge rectangular hole in the ground, half-filled with the blackened, water-soaked remains of the building which had collapsed onto itself. It wasn't the first heap of remains left by a twisted individual who apparently took some kind of perverse pleasure in destroying the adopted homes of elderly persons no longer able to care for themselves.

Chief Dunn and Chief Smythe-Bates each undertook searching the areas that best fit their field of expertise. Dunn began at the edge of the woods surrounding the clearing in which the destroyed building had been centered and circled inward.

Smythe-Bates started at the edge of the wreckage and slowly circled the dead building outward, watching closely for clues until the men met at the far end by the greasy, still-wet asphalt parking lot. Smythe-Bates said: "I didn't see a thing but wet dirt, did you see anything?" Dunn answered: "A couple of footprints close to the door by the far end of the building. But they could be from anybody; a staff member, or even a visitor." The Police Chief said: "Staff perhaps, but quite unlikely a visitor. A visitor would not have used the door on the other end of the building from the parking lot." He started walking toward his car. "Where are you going?" Dunn asked surprised. "I was going to the station to get the moulage kit I saw in the store-room so I might make a plaster cast of the prints you found." Then he paused and asked Dunn, "Wait, do you have a smart phone? He patted his own pocket. "Mine is with a service provider in the U.K. It probably won't get a signal here, or if it did, the roaming charges would be astronomically high." "Sure." Dunn chuckled and pulled a phone from his pocket and tossed it to Smythe-Bates. "What are you going to do with it?" With a smile, Smythe-Bates said, "Don't worry, I won't ring up my cousin in Singapore."

"Show me the footprints you found so I can snap a few pictures of them; it's cleaner and easier than the plaster." Dunn said, "You don't need to be connected to a cell-service to take pictures," "I know, said Smythe-Bates. But I'd like very much to send copies to the police station, and for that to happen, it does have to be connected."

"Gotcha." The Fire Chief nodded and pointed toward the far end of the hole in the ground that used to be a building and said, "That way."

Smythe-Bates followed him to where a pair of sneaker prints had pressed into the muddy soil. The Police Chief squatted over the prints and said, "It's a shame they were so degraded by the water while the fire was being extinguished."

"It's hard to keep things dry when you're fighting a building fire. The idea is to move as much water as possible, as fast as possible. But this place was mostly gone when we arrived on scene."

"I don't doubt it a bit. Smythe-Bates peered down at the prints: "However, there's still some useful information here."

"Like what" Questioned Dunn. "Well, I'd estimate they are size ten…and there's that." The Police Chief pointed to the left sneaker print. "Stevie Wonder wouldn't have miss that clue." Dunn slapped his forehead. "Damn it, I missed the swoosh; they're obviously Nikes. Forgive me, I'm not a famous detective, just a lowly hose jockey." Then after a moment's pause, he added, "Will that really be much help? I mean even in a little town like this, there must be a hundred people wearing Nikes."

Smythe-Bates pointed at the right sneaker print and said: "Whoever our firebug is, he probably has a bad right ankle." Dunn seemed confused:

"How do you figure?" The Police Chief responded: "The sole is worn down much more on the outside. Probably from an old break that didn't heal properly, or possibly a bad sprain." Dunn quipped "Are you a doctor, too?"

Chief Symthe-Bates replied:

"No", but I have had a broken ankle and it still occasionally hurts like hell. Not to mention that right print helps in another way. There's a nail or tack in the sole.

We find the shoe that matches that print and we've got our man." Chief Dunn asked: "So are we going to stop every man we see wearing what looks like a size ten Nike and check his shoes?" Chief Smythe-Bates replied: "No, but when we have an actual suspect…"

"It'll be one more piece of evidence to get him" Dunn finished his thought. "Right the first time" nodded Smythe-Bates

The police chief stepped back and shaded his eyes from the lowering sun in the west. Then he nodded toward the Fire Chief's bright red SUV with a red bubble-gum light on top and Town of Martin's Grove - Fire Department decal on the side. "Do you happen to have a ladder in there?" Dunn shook his head: "No, when I go out there are always plenty of ladders around. Why?"

"I see something that needs a closer look." He pointed down into the hole in the ground and then asked: "Was the door on this end of the building closest to the kitchen where the fire started?" "Yeah, according to the floor plan, we're right over where the kitchen was located."

"Okay, I've got to get down there; do you have any ideas?"

"The fire chief answered, somewhat hesitantly: "I have a rope in the van and you look pretty spindly. I think I can handle your weight but you'd still be taking a hell of a chance. It's a good fourteen feet to the bottom and it's covered with all kinds of rubble. There's everything from burned lumber to the kitchen sink, literally. It damn sure wouldn't be a comfortable landing if the rope snapped. Are you sure you that you want to do this?" The Police Chief nodded: "They say nothing ventured, nothing gained."

"I say, nothing ventured, nothing fractured." Dunn sarcastically replied: "Hold on a few seconds." As Dunn went to his van and retrieved a coil of stout-looking rope. He draped it over his shoulder and found a tactical flashlight bringing the both to Smythe-Bates. "You know, your health insurance probably hasn't even kicked in yet." Then he added, "If you're determined to do this, let's use some common sense." Dunn glanced over the edge into the pit. "What do you have in mind?" Dunn said: "Just stay put until I pull the van around. I'm going to put the bumper right here," He drew a line in the dirt with the toe of his boot. "I'll tie the rope to it. I know I called you spindly, but accidents do happen. Four new Firestones are less likely to slip than my worn-out old boots." He jogged away around the building and in less than a minute, the van's engine fired up and its headlights came into view, flooding he area with bright light. He positioned the van's front bumper almost exactly above the line he'd scratched in the ground.

Hopping out, he walked to the Police Chief and said:

"Okay, if you're absolutely sure you want to do this, we're going to do it as safely as possible." Quickly and expertly, he made a slip knot in the rope and fashioned a lasso-like loop in the end. "Are you expecting a herd of wild horses?" the Police Chief asked. "Nope." Wise-cracked Dunn. "Well, what do you plan on lassoing?" "Just one loony, limey Police Chief; reach for the sky Copper." Dunn lifted his head skyward as he said it, a big grin on his face."

Smythe-Bates replied: "You do know you're quite insane, don't you?" Dunn snickered: "I'm not the one getting ready to swing on a rope into a concrete ditch full of dangerous shit waiting to impaled."

The Police Chief raised his arms: "Point taken."

The Fire Chief put the loop in the rope over his extended arms and lowered it to just below his arm-pits. Then he snugged up the loop, and asked, "Too tight?"

The Police Chief grimaced a little: "No, I believe it will be adequate, now what is the plan?"

Dunn looped the rope around the van's bumper and said: "Whenever you're ready, just back over the edge, real slow." He paused and pointed at a tall soot covered brick chimney jutting up at least thirty feet from the rubble-strewn basement. "See that?"

"Affirmative" the police chief answered. "Well," Dunn continued, "When you go over the edge and start down, I'll begin easing the van forward. And I *do* mean easing. It'll be in gear, but the engine will be idling with my foot on the brake. I'll be watching that chimney. Flash the light on it every time you think you've dropped about another five feet. When you're almost to the bottom, flash the light on it twice; I'll be watching it real close. And if things go really bad, fire off a shot with that hog-leg." Dunn grinned and pointed at the gun the new police chief had on his hip. "I don't think I've seen you with that before.

Is that standard issue for Scotland Yard inspectors?" The Chief smiled: "No, but I thought it suited my new location; don't you agree?"

"Yeah, no better side-arm for a New Mexico lawman than a Colt 45, Dunn replied: And a chrome one at that. Then he added: I thought British cops didn't carry guns."

"You've been watching too many old movies. Although I will admit, a Colt six-shooter wasn't what I carried in London. To be brutally honest, finding one of those firearms anywhere in the UK would have been quite difficult."

Dunn snickered. "Not a problem here, huh?"

"Indeed not. There are at least ten establishments in this hamlet where you can buy one in five minutes." Dunn laughed: "Welcome to the American west." The police chief said: "Let's get on with it." He looked over the edge into the blackened pit, gave Dunn a thumbs-up as he sat behind the wheel of the van and then getting a firm, two-handed grip on the rope and looking over his shoulder, he eased back over the edge.

He began essentially walking backward down the wall, constantly glancing over his shoulder, then down between his legs to judge how far and fast he was descending and what he was descending upon. Every few moments when he surmised he'd dropped about five feet he flashed the light on the chimney to notify Chief Dunn. When he'd nearly touched bottom, he flashed the chimney twice quickly and then heard Dunn give the van's engine a brief rev before it fell silent.

Smythe-Bates pulled the slip-knot loose and took the loop of the rope from around his waist...

Dunn had barely stepped from the van when he heard the loud roar of a pistol shot boom up from the rubble-strewn foundation.

He ran to the edge of the pit and shouted: "You okay?"

"Yeah, but I believe I am about half deaf. This damn thing is loud! Were all of the gunfighters in the old West hard of hearing?"

Then the Police Chief started to laugh uncontrollably. Dunn wasn't amused: "I said fire a shot if something went really bad." In between chuckles the Police Chief replied: "It was really bad."

"What was?" demanded Chief Dunn."

Smythe-Bates said, "That was," and shone his light into the corner of the demolished kitchen. Then he said: "At least it sounded really bad when I heard it growling in the dark. When I put my torch on it, all I could see was its yellow eyes shining in the blackness. They didn't look any friendlier than the growl sounded.

When it started coming toward me, I pulled off a shot."

He stepped closer to the dead animal and put the flashlight closer to its face. "I suppose it's a wolf, whatever it is, it's quite big, and thankfully quite dead." the fire chief whistled. "That's not a wolf, it's a coyote. It must have been nosing through the canned meats that burst open from the heat of the fire. You're right, it is a big one and you plugged that sucker right between the eyes. Nice shootin' Tex!" In a horrible British accented southern Texas draw, Police Chief Smythe

-Bates remarked: "Aw shucks, it wurn't nuthin." Ditching the Texas slang, he continued: "I did find what I spotted from up there, give me a minute to dig it out then you can pull me out of here. Do you have a shovel? I could do it with a board but that would take a while; I've enjoyed about all I can stand of this hole."

Dunn laughed. "Yeah, there's one in the van, I won't take a minute."

"Good, I'd rather not meet any more New Mexico wildlife." A moment later Dunn called out, "Heads up!"

"Ready." Smythe-Bates stepped back as a folded camp shovel careened down, hitting the floor of the foundation. "Thanks, got it!" the Police Chief called up. "Good, let me know when you're ready."

"It'll only take a minute or two. It's not very big but I won't have any way to hold it while you're pulling me back up. Have you got any ideas?"

"Would a plastic grocery bag do? I've got one in the van."

"Sounds perfect." A few seconds later a white plastic bag

came floating down. The Police Chief yelled "Thanks, I'll get started. It won't take long. I'll let you know when I'm ready. I want to get out of here before the sun goes down any more."

"I can't say as I blame you." Dunn acknowledged. A few minutes later, he heard the Police Chief shout: "I'm ready any time dear sir, let's get this show on the road!"

Dunn asked: "You got the rope wrapped around you?"

The van's engine fired up, the rope drew taught, and Edwin Smythe-Bates walked up the soot-caked concrete wall into the glare of the van's headlights.

When they were seated in the van the fire chief said, "What's our next move?"

The Police Chief said: "Let's go back to the station and I'll show you what I found."

"Which station, yours or mine?" Dunn asked. Smythe-Bates shrugged dramatically "I don't really care but I most certainly could use a pint or two.

Would you happen to have any lager at your shop?" Dunn grinned. "I just happen to have twelve in the reefer and they're ice cold. I hope that's okay because I've heard you Brits drink it warm."

"That's simply a myth, much like British police officers not carrying guns." Snapped Smythe-Bates. "I like it cold and I suppose twelve will have to do."

Twenty minutes later, the Chiefs were seated at the old scarred-up table in the fire house kitchen, each with a frosted bottle of Lone-Star beer. The badly -scorched item the

Police Chief had retrieved from the ruins of the burned-out retirement home sat on the table. Dunn asked: "So that's it? Looks like an old fashioned windup alarm clock."

"Righto old man." chimed the Police Chief. "It's an I.I.D." Correcting him, Dunn replied: "Don't you mean I. E. D?" Shaking his head, Smythe-Bates explained: "No no, it's not an improvised explosive device, it's an improvised incendiary device. It doesn't explode, it starts a fire."

"Well, how in the living hell does it do that Mr., Eddie?" Chief Dunn hung his head: "Saying that name will take some getting used to." Smythe-Bates rolled his eyes: "Not nearly as much as it will me hearing it. Actually, it's one of the simplest timers ever, and one of the most common. You wind the clock, and set it for the time you want your explosion to go off or fire to start. Then if you prefer to not have the alarm be heard, you wrap the little clappers that strike the bell with masking tape to silence them. If it's to be hidden and not in area where it might be heard, then that's unnecessary. You wind a length of string or fishing tackle around the winding key and hook the other end to a switch. Lay the clock face down so the key is free to turn. When the clock reaches the alarm time and starts to ring, the key tightens up the string and pulls the switch. The switch closes a circuit on a battery and you get a bang or a spark. Chief Duun seems mesmerized.

"Wow, that's so simple I can't believe I've never heard of it." Smythe-Bates nodded. "Don't be surprised, things like that are rampant on the internet. I'm intimately aware of the process because Brandon Winston used it quite often."

"Brandon who?" asked Dunn. "The Soho Torcher" replied the Police Chief.

On the ride to the station from the site of the last nursing home fire, they decided since they would be spending considerable time together cooperating on the case. It turned out that they *both* liked their beer cold and first names

seemed appropriate. As they drank their first beer together, now the fire chief was Lenny, and the police chief was Eddie. Chief Smythe-Bates looked puzzled:

"Is something wrong?" Chief Dunn grinned. "No, but you just don't look like an Eddie. Frankly you really do seem more like an Edwin, or at least Ed. Maybe it's the accent."

"You should be flattered my new American friend. Even the people that I was close to at The Yard called me Ed. Only my wife calls me Eddie, and my Mum, before she passed." Lenny pouted. Really, so why am I so honored?"

"You did lower me into a miniature pit from hell without letting me get killed.

CHAPTER 4

Care-Haven Acres

The grounds surrounding the vast L-shaped main building at Care-Haven Acres retirement home more closely resembled an Ivy-League college campus than the properties that had held the town's other four nursing homes, now all reduced to piles of blackened debris. The winding driveway leading up to the facility was laid with cut flagstone and a large, ornate wrought-iron gate magically slid open, via motion activation. Leonard Dunn pulled his fire-engine-red SUV onto the property and the big gate closed smoothly and quietly. Edwin Smythe-Bates rolled his eyes and said: "If this were London, I'd assume royalty resides inside. I find it difficult to believe this palatial estate sits in a little town like this."

Dunn answered: "No, not royalty, just the area's most financially well-off retired folks." Then he added: "Martin's Grove isn't that small for a desert town in New Mexico. There are towns close by that are nothing more than a gas pump and a speed bump. The Police Chief looked around the posh grounds and said: "Very well, if you say so." Dunn asked: "Okay, are we ready Detective?"

"I'm as ready as I can be." Smythe-Bates chimed, picking up his clipboard. "I've got my checklist."

"Dunn patted his jacket pocket and said: "Good, let's get this over with."

The town's two Chiefs, Fire and Police, entered Care-Haven Acres' large main building, equipped to perform a thorough check of the premises' fire and security systems. The entry hall was every bit as grand as the property surrounding the facility. The massive foyer nearly as large as the truck bay at the fire station.

The floor was white tile, immaculately polished. It shone like a mirror in the sunlight from the floor-to-ceiling windows. A pair of 19th century crystal chandeliers hung from the vaulted ceiling, easily thirty feet above the floor.

When they had taken less than a dozen steps from the door, a chime sounded. The Tone was low and mellow. Suddenly a man in a tailored gray pin-stripe suit with a black bolo tie appeared from a corridor on the far side of the room. The two Chiefs looked at each other and shrugged, clearly confused.

The stranger in the suit said: "The motion sensor alerted me of your presence. Who are you two gentlemen, and how may I be of assistance?"

Caught up in the moment, and playing to a crowd of one, Leonard Dunn bowed slightly and said: "I'm Leonard Dunn, the town's Fire Chief, and this distinguished gentleman is Edwin Smythe-Bates, Martin's Grove's new Chief of Police." The sharp-dressed man replied:

"Well that certainly explains your both being in uniform."

"We're here to check out your extraordinarily gorgeous

facility's fire warning and suppression systems as well as security readiness in light of recent events affecting businesses of your sort in our area," Dunn finished with a flourish."The man seemed on the verge of crying: "Oh, thank goodness, I've been nearly scared to death these past few weeks." Dunn told the man: "There's a distinct possibility you might hear an alarm sound as we're inspecting the building. If so, please don't worry. It will be us conducting tests. Please notify your guests and staff to be aware it could happen and remind them not to panic."

Dunn again bowed slightly and said: "If you'd be kind enough to direct us toward your kitchen and storage areas so we can get on about our business."The man bowed: "I'd be happy to show you."

The police chief answered, "That's kind of you, but I'm sure you are a busy man.

If you would be so kind as to point us in the right direction, we'll be just fine."

"Of course." As he pointed at a door across the room. As they walked across the opulent entryway towards the door the man in the five-hundred-dollar suit had indicated, Smythe-Bates said: "Lenny, there's a word we use in law enforcement back in the U. K. that describes you to a tee, but you may not be familiar with it."

Dunn looked puzzled. "Really, what word is that?"The Police Chief giggled:

"Nuts." Dunn revealed a wide grin. "It's an old habit. Eddie, I try to make at least one person smile each day.

Obviously, it didn't work with that guy but I think some people are born without smile-muscles. They get jobs as greeters in places like this."

As they approached the door, the Police Chief again looked around the lavish entry hall and said: "I didn't have a chance to look at any of the other four homes before they burned, but I saw plenty of photographs; enough to make it

obvious that this place is on a whole different level." Dunn said: "Sadly, all men may be created equal but they don't all die equal. Remember the story Mayor Poole told you about the mayor back in the sixties who was a merchandising whiz and sold the town as a get-well-quick/cure-all location?"

"Yes, I remember."

"Well, selling the town wasn't the only thing he was good at. Did you see the huge Ford and Lincoln dealership north of town?" Smythe-Bates lifted one eyebrow.

"How could I miss it?" Well, the mayor who sold this town's reputation also sold Fords. He was as good at selling cars as he was at convincing people that our climate would work wonders for whatever ailed them. So, a lot of sick people moved in. When some of them got well they couldn't wait to tell the world it was because of our climate...and maybe some of it was true. Damned if I know. I'm no doctor. I'm just a hose-jockey. But the town kept growing and the mayor kept getting richer. The people who moved in had kids and grandkids. The more a town grows, the more residents grow old. That mayor's grandson owns the Ford dealership now, and also this place." The fire chief waved his hand around them to indicate the room they stood in. "Yeah, the wealthy own it and pretty much only the wealthy, or at least the well-off, can afford to stay here." Chief Smythe-Bates said: "I didn't realize Martin's Grove had that many wealthy people."

"Eddie, in our little corner of the world, wealth is relative. It's true there aren't many businesses that pay big salaries here in town, but Santa Fe is only a couple hours away. If someone doesn't mind spending some time commuting, they can do okay. A guy or gal who spends four hours a day driving round-trip to Santa Fe to work as a ticket agent at the airport and can make twice what they'd make working at Target here might consider themselves wealthy, especially if it comes to the point that his parents need long-term care."

The Police Chief lamented: "You know Lenny, you're more of a deep-thinker than I realized, maybe you're only a little bit nuts." Chief Dunn tilted his head: "I don't know about that; please don't underestimate me!"

The well-dressed greeter had pointed them towards an opening on a hallway that stretched the length of the shorter leg of the building's L shape. It was well-marked with signs that hung from the ceiling to indicate which way to go in order to reach various and important areas of the huge facility. Dunn said: "If this place was any bigger, they'd need a lighted map with an arrow saying You-Are-Here, like at a shopping mall." The signs they were both interested in said Service and Staff Entrances and Kitchen and Food Prep. The arrows on both signs pointed down the hall in the same direction. Looking in the direction the signs they could see a door at the far end with a red security bar across it that held a sign which read: Emergency Exit Only/Alarm Will Sound. The fire chief said: "Eddie, I'd bet a dollar that door opens on the employee parking lot, and it's also where they take deliveries. And that means that's just where our guy is most likely to strike, if he follows his pattern. That other sign says the kitchen is down this way too. So far, he's picked kitchens as his initial fire starting places." Chief Smythe-Bates asked: "Why do you think that is? You are certainly the fire expert."

Chief Dunn replied: "Kitchens are always full of flammable things, lots of paper and cloth.

Sometimes, when they're not cleaned properly, there's a lot of grease and oil left behind that acts as an accelerant. That's good for the bad guys and really bad for the good guys. But I don't really think that's the issue here." The Police Chief agreed: "Probably not; the floor looks clean enough to eat off of." Then he looked down the hall: "Well, that's impressive." Dunn squinted: "What's impressive?"

Chief Smythe-Bates pointed along the ceiling." Chief Dunn raised his eyebrows:

"Wow, I never saw so many cameras in one hallway; looks like the lobby of a bank." A row of shiny-new cameras, a dozen feet apart, ran along the full length of the wall on one side of the hall, about a foot down from the ceiling. "Earlier I called the manager and told him to get really serious about security. This guy certainly came through. I'll call the company that installed the system and find out more about it as soon as I get back to my office." Chief Smythe-Bates asked: "Do you have any idea who might have installed these cameras?"

"Not yet." Piped Dunn. "But we passed a sign with their name and number on the way in; I'll check it as we leave. Wow Eddie, you detectives don't miss a trick, do you?"

The Police Chief grinned: "No Lenny, but that is why I am occasionally paid handsomely."

Chief Dunn chuckled: Okay Sherlock, let's go see if they were as thorough on their fire suppression systems."

They moved on to the kitchen and storage areas where the previous fires had originated. Their examination of this kitchen however, offered no surprises. It was as clean and well organized as the rest of the facility. The Fire Chief was especially impressed by the number of smoke and heat detectors in the kitchen, as well as numerous fire extinguishers. As they left the kitchen, Dunn pointed left toward the emergency door at the end of the hall and said: "Eddie, let's go out that way instead of the way we came in." Chief Smythe-Bates frowned: "Why?" Chief Dunn explained: "Well, that door's closer to the kitchen so if our fire-starter tries to break in, that's probably where he'll enter. Also, there's something I want to take a look at near that exit."

"Very well" said the Police Chief, "A walk around the building won't hurt me. I've read that exercise is a good thing."

When they got a couple dozen feet from the emergency exit Dunn said, "You see that, Eddie?" He pointed toward a gray rectangular metal door about two-feet wide by three-feet high set into the wall about six feet off the floor. "That's an emergency unit in case of fire." Chief Smythe-Bates looked puzzled. "I thought they were always encased in glass with a sign that said: IN CASE OF FIRE–BREAK GLASS?"

The Fire Chief grinned and said: "Not this kind." Slipping his finger in the thin space between the top of the door and the wall above it, he manipulated the hatch until a click came from behind the door. It popped open about an inch and Chief Dunn grabbed the edge and swung it the rest of the way open.

Smythe-Bates snickered: "Bloody well-done Lenny! I had no idea you were a magician. That was a cracking good discovery!" Dunn downplayed: "It's not magic, just part of the job. I go through yearly courses to stay up on how equipment works." He pointed into the cavity behind the door. Behind it was a large metal spool with a flattened braided hose wrapped around it. It was tipped with a cone-shaped brass nozzle. A large lever-handled valve was next to it.

"Brilliant and incredibly cool, but why is the latch hidden?" asked the Police Chief.

"That's simple Eddie. It's designed so only fire-fighters know how to access it.

The hose is only eight feet long, but when you open that valve, the water comes out hard and fast enough to just about peel the paint from that emergency exit door.

But it's also enough to slam a person against a wall, and I mean hard. That's not something just anybody should be able to gain access into." Smythe-Bates nodded: "That makes perfect sense to me." Dunn smiled and said: "That's nice to hear because I hardly ever make perfect sense."

They walked the rest of the way to the emergency exit and Dunn reached for the safety bar. Challenging him, the Police Chief raised his voice: "Are you going to push that mechanism? Won't that trigger the alarm?"

Dunn nodded: "It's the only way to be a hundred percent sure it's functional. Hopefully the well-dressed robot who greeted us earlier kept his word and warned staff members this might happen." He pushed the bar and the door swung outward. A loud alarm bell rang overhead. Immediately, a voice they recognized as the greeter's sounded from several large wall-mounted speakers explaining it was a false alarm and there was no need for concern and instructing all guests to remain in their rooms until further notice.

Smythe-Bates asked Dunn: "Well, are you satisfied?" Dunn seemed satisfied: "Yeah, a lot of this gear is old, possibly bought refurbished, but it all appears to be in fine shape. If you're ready Eddie, let's get the hell outta here."

As they slowly cruised out the long driveway, Dunn paused by the sign they'd seen on the way in. Police Chief Smythe-Bates read it aloud: "Sensel Security Specialists "Nice alliteration, huh?" He made a note of the name and phone number, and thought: "I shall call them as soon as we get back to the office."

CHAPTER 5

Miss Betty – Introduction

The Fire and Police Chiefs' impressions regarding Care-Haven Acres were spot-on. It had been designed by an architect with over a dozen luxury hotels on his résumé. The furniture and drapes were top of the line. The place was designed and built with the purpose of attracting clientele not as much from the local area but from as far away as Santa Fe or Albuquerque. It was a high-dollar facility for well-off clients. Not only were the rooms beautiful, but no expense was spared in other areas. The hallways featured floral gold-leaf wallpaper. Door frames and window-sills were walnut, and polished to a high sheen, as were the chair-rails, 38 inches above the brightly buffed floors. The doors to each guest room displayed a number for the convenience of visitors. Each door also had a narrow gold-colored horizontal track which showed the last name of the guest who currently occupied the room. It was a way for visitors to double check that they were in the right place before possibly knocking on the wrong door and disturbing someone unnecessarily. Room 108 was the residence of Mrs. Betty Peacemaker, a stately woman only fifteen months away from her ninetieth birthday. Like every other room, the door to 108 held the room number, but instead of the name Peacemaker in the placeholder, it had been replaced by an embossed care that read Miss Betty. Below that, someone had taped a carefully hand-lettered 3x5 card that read:

Blessed are the peacemakers, for they shall be called children of God.

The day after the day the two Chiefs performed their inspection of the preparedness of Care-Haven Acres, the Police Chief received a call from the owner of the home requesting that the two men come in some time and hold a short question-and-answer style meeting with the home's residents. The caller hoped it might ease the resident's anxiety over what they had read in the paper or seen on the TV news about the recent arsons. He promised to talk to the Fire Chief and schedule something as soon as possible. Two evenings later, on Friday at 7:00 pm, the well-dressed man who had initially greeted both Chiefs stood at a small podium in the front of Care-Haven-Acres' beautifully decorated social hall. He nervously leaned closer than necessary to the microphone before him and after whispering, "Test, test," spoke a little louder. "Good-evening ladies and gentlemen. Thank you for coming. These two uniformed gentlemen, Mr. Leonard Dunn, Martin's Grove's Fire Chief , and Mr. Edwin Smythe-Bates, Martin's Grove's new Police Chief have graciously found time to come this evening and talk with us." He gestured toward each man as he said his name. "They are ready to answer any questions or concerns you may have. Please raise your hand if you have a question and wait to be recognized so we can have an orderly meeting." He looked at the two guests: "Are you ready gentlemen?" They both nodded. Immediately an elderly white-haired lady sitting front-and center raised her hand. The greeter, acting as a moderator said, "Yes ma'am." Although her hand had trembled slightly in the air, in a strong clear voice the lady asked: "Chief Smythe-Bates, aren't you the detective who caught the Soho Torcher?" Struggling with the effort he was expending to contain his urge to laugh, Dunn looked at the police chief and shrugged. Finally, at a loss for words, Chief Smythe-Bates said: "Indeed I am Ma'am. Now, since you know my name, I think it's only fair for me to know yours?" He winked as he asked the question. "I suppose so, young man. My name is Betty Peacemaker and I am pleased to make your acquaintance." The Police Chief tipped an imaginary hat and said: "The pleasure is all mine. I am curious, how do you know about the Soho torcher?"

"That's simple" she replied, matter-of-factly. "I have friends in high places. Your name seemed familiar when I read it in the newspaper so I called one of those friends and he looked you up for me." Being extremely polite, Chief Smythe-Bates asked: "Now I'm curious, Miss Peacemaker, or is it Mrs?"

"Mrs. Peacemaker. My husband passed on ten years ago; is that what you were curious about?" she asked with a slightly sarcastic tone. "No ma'am" quipped the Police Chief. "I was wondering more about your friend in a high place." The white-haired lady winked: "Oh, he's the head librarian in Santa Fe. Smythe-Bates countered: "And you consider that a high place? No offence my lady,"

"Of course. His office is on the top floor and everybody knows every town's library has the most stories of any building in town." A few scattered laughs and some applause popped up among the crowd gathered in the social hall. The greeter said: "Thank you Miss Betty for providing this evening's entertainment." The white-haired lady flashed a beautiful smile and looking directly at Chief Dunn she winked again: "Pleasure to see you again, Leonard." Dunn blushed a little: "It's wonderful to see you too Miss Betty. It's been way too long. I didn't know you were staying here." She shifted in her chair: "Everybody ends up somewhere Leonard. Better here than pushing up daisies. That will come soon enough." Now now Mrs. Peacemaker, don't talk like that." Dunn replied firmly. The greeter spoke up, "Does anyone have any pertinent questions for our guests?" A man several rows back cleared his throat and raised his hand. The Police Chief said: "Yes sir?" The man continued: "If I understand correctly, four of the town's five retirement homes have been burned to the ground and this is the only one remaining. Is that correct?" The Chief nodded: "Yes sir, I'm afraid it is."

"I don't know why you're afraid" the man in the crowd countered. "You're not the one living at ground zero of some wacko's plan. Are you doing anything about it? Do you have any clues?" Smythe-Bates drew a deep calming breath and said: "Actually sir, we've received what I believe to be a promising tip just this orning. Information has been sent to the New Mexico State Police and the Federal Bureau of Investigation. You can be sure that this place is being closely monitored **_day and night_** by people from both my department and Chief Dunn's. We also recovered a key piece of evidence from the last arson site that gives us a clear picture of how the perpetrator operates. Knowing what to look for always is a big plus, as I'm sure you can imagine." Chief Dunn spoke up, "May I interject something?" The greeter nodded. "As far as I'm concerned, you're welcome to do so Chief."

"Thank you. I'm not a native of Martin's Grove, but I've lived here since graduating from high school. I'm about as close to being from here as you can be without being born here. I care a lot about the town and its people. All of its people, people of any age. I haven't known Chief Smythe-Bates very long, but it didn't take long for me to decide that he's the right man for this job. I'd trust him with my life and you can trust him with yours. Still standing, Betty Peacemaker turned to face the crowd and in that same strong steady voice said "If Leonard Dunn says it, that's good enough of ascent passed through the assembled group". Not necessarily a show of confidence in the new Police Chief, but a clear show of confidence in the wisdom and discretion of Betty Peacemaker.

As soon as it was clear that things were calm, the greeter leaned into the microphone and said: "It appears our guests have answered almost any questions that I can imagine coming up, I'll take this moment to remind everyone that very shortly there will be light refreshments and a time for informal socializing and discussion in the back of the hall." He turned to the two men on stage and asked, "Do you gentlemen mind staying for a short while?" Both men replied that they'd be happy to stay and accompanied by the sounds of metal chairs being folded and numerous feet shuffling across the shiny tile floor, they made their way through the shrinking crowd toward a long folding table in the rear of the hall. Chief

Smythe-Bates was more than a little uncomfortable when he spotted the man who had pressed him hard for firm promises he wasn't able to give standing in line for refreshments. The man's face already wore an unpleasant scowl. Chief Dunn's reception was much more delightful. As he neared the group at the snack-and-drink table, Betty Peacemaker stepped towards him, put her arms around him and said: "God love you Leonard, it's delightful to see you!" Bending slightly and being careful not to squeeze too hard, the Fire Chief returned her hug. "Right back at you, Miss Betty." His smile was so wide the Police Chief wondered what kept the top of his head from popping off. He smiled at the two of them and said: "My keen detective instincts tell me that you two have met before. Is that a private story, or is it one you'd like to share?" The lady nodded toward the police chief and said: "I like him Leonard. You sure know how to pick your friends." Dunn gave her a peck on the cheek and said: "I always have." She smiled, but a tear rolled down her cheek. Then she asked: "Why don't you two come to my room and we can explain to the Police Chief how we became acquainted? I'm in room 108." Chief Dunn grinned and said: "Now Miss Betty, aren't you afraid people will talk?" She bristled: "The hell with them! I'm single and over eighteen. Actually, I'm almost seventy-two years over eighteen. I'd say that makes it my business who I choose to socialize with. How about the two of you stopping by my room at six-thirty, just in time for *Jeopardy;* I never miss it. Remember now, room 108." Leonard Dunn said: "Yes Ma'am, we'll be there, I promise. The police chief added, sincerely: "I wouldn't miss it for the world." Miss Betty favored them with a smile and a lady-like finger wave and headed out the door into the hall.

An attractive woman in a uniform with a stethoscope draped around her neck came up to the two Chiefs and introduced herself: "I'm Sandi VanMetre. I'm the head nurse here at the home. Did I hear you say you're going to Miss Betty's room for Jeopardy?" Chief Dunn smiled and nodded. "That's right, why do you ask?" The nurse snickered and said, "If you play against her, be prepared to be embarrassed. On Monday evenings, a bunch of the guests and staff gather in her room to play Jeopardy against her, sometimes there are a dozen of us in all. At first the management wanted to make us stop but it did so much good for everybody's mood they decided to let us keep participating. There's a calendar on the bulletin board in the kitchen where we put our initials if we beat her. That calendar sometimes goes two months without a mark. She's a very rare lady: wise *and* smart." Leonard grinned and said, "Tell me something I don't know."

CHAPTER 6

Jeopardy

At 6:25, the Fire and Police chiefs stood just outside room 108. Leonard Dunn rapped on the door and called out: "Miss Betty?" The lady's now

familiar voice came from inside. "The door is open, please come on in! I'm

dressed. With the type of work you men do, you probably wouldn't be traumatized even if I wasn't dressed. You've both no-doubt seen wrinkles before. When they entered the room, Betty said: "Well, I should have had you come by earlier, it's damn near Jeopardy time. We'll have to wait until after the show to explain our past history to the new Police Chief, won't we Leonard?"

"That's fine with me Miss Betty", Dunn answered. "How about you, Eddie?"

"Not a problem." Replied the curious Police Chief. Betty boosted herself into a sitting position in the bed and said: "You two pull up chairs and I'll call room-service." As the two men pulled visitor's chairs closer to the bed, she pushed a button on the nurse call-box. A voice answered immediately: "Yes, Miss Betty? Is there something you need?"

Betty looked at the two Chiefs and raised an eyebrow. "Coffee or a soda maybe?"

Smythe-Bates shook his head, Dunn said, "Coffee would be nice." Betty said into the box, "Could we have a coffee for Chief Dunn please?" "Anything else Miss Betty?"

"Yes. I'm feeling a little worn out. Do you think I might have a Gatorade? That is, of course, unless you have a Bud Light." The voice on the other end replied, "Miss Betty, you're a card. And oh, would it be okay if I came in for Jeopardy with you, too."

"Yeah, I'm a real joker. Of course, come on in, the more the merrier." Then she pushed another button on the box and Johnny Gilbert's amplified voice announced: "*This Is Jeopardy!*"

A few minutes later a nurse's aide arrived with a cup of coffee and a bottle of Gatorade. She apologized: "Sorry, Miss Betty, no Bud Light tonight. Hope you don't mind that a few of the others are coming along, I hope that's okay."

"Sure, but no beer, huh?" Betty shrugged and said: "Oh, well, it's like Mick said back in '65…I can't get no satisfaction." On the TV Johnny Gilbert said: "And now, here's the host of Jeopardy, Ken Jennings." Chief Dunn asked, "What do you think of him, Miss Betty?" She tilted her head a little. "Who, young Ken?"

"Yes." Asked Dunn. She said: "I think he's a very brave young man. Can you imagine how he must have felt the first time he was introduced by Johnny Gilbert as the host of Jeopardy? He must have felt like Lyndon Johnson did the first time he was introduced as The President of the United States.

It must be scary being expected to replace the irreplaceable." Chief Smythe-Bates interrupted: "Miss Betty, you are exactly as advertised: wise *and* smart." She seemed to blush: "Thank you Chief. That compliment seems particularly kind spoken with your lovely accent." Now the Police Chief felt warm and slightly embarrassed: "You are more than welcome, Miss Betty." Miss Betty said, "The game's starting." By then there were a half-dozen people in the room. It took two clues in two categories to prove to the Chiefs they were in over their heads if they hoped to compete with this lady. In the category 'Children's Literature' the clue was: This best-seller was written using only fifty words as the result of a challenge from a publisher to the author. "What is 'Green Eggs and Ham?'" Miss Betty blurted out immediately. None of the contestants on the screen knew the answer. Later, in the double jeopardy round, in the category 'Rock and Roll Firsts', to the clue: He was the first former Beatle to have a number one hit after the band's split. The names John and Paul flew around room 108. One nurse even said, "Who is Ringo Starr?"

Miss Betty answered, "Who was George Harrison?" Her answer brought surprised looks from the group of people in her room. When it was confirmed by Ken Jennings, she merely grinned and said, "My Sweet Lord." Leonard Dunn laughed and said: "That nurse, Miss VanMetre wasn't kidding when she said we'd be embarrassed playing Jeopardy with you Miss Betty."

"Don't take it too hard Leonard. I've had a lot more years to absorb trivia than you have." "It's not just the absorbing that's amazing. It's the recalling. You amazed me years ago, and you still do." Smythe-Bates said, "Okay, this mystery is getting to be too much for me." Miss Betty glanced at her bedside clock and said, "The show will be over in ten minutes, and then I'll tell you the story, I promise."

"I'm counting on it young lady" The Police Chief pointed to her. She dropped him a wink. "It's a promise."

As it turned out Miss Betty and Chief Dunn both shared in explaining their past relationship. Miss Betty started by saying: "Leonard and I met at South Central High School in Santa Fe." Chief Smythe-Bates interrupted again. "If you'll forgive me for saying, you two don't look close enough in age to have gotten your yearbooks in the same year." Dunn said, "I was a student, and Miss Betty was the assistant principal, and also the guidance counselor. She's also the reason I got into fire-fighting."

"Really?" Asked the Police Chief. "In the U.K.. civil service and first-responder type professions aren't usually included in career counseling."

"That's not exactly how it went down. " Miss Betty corrected. Chief Dunn nodded. "No, not at all." Betty pressed the nurse-station call button again.

When the unit clerk answered, she asked: "I'm sorry to be a bother my dear, but my guests and I were about to get into a gab session that might run a bit long. Would it be an end-of-the-world-level offence if we went past the normal visiting hours?" The reply came immediately: "Miss Betty, as far as I'm concerned you, can entertain your guests as long as you like. If it were up to me, I'd give you the keys to this place and let you lock the place up at the end of the day." Betty laughed: "You'd better be careful talking like that or you'll have these two good-looking young men thinking I can walk on water. The big boss might not like it if he heard you talking that way either." The voice on the other end replied: "I'll risk it ma'am. What that man needs is a lesson about what the real world is like for real people; those who weren't born with a silver spoon so far down their throat that the toilet paper rubs against it when they wipe." Betty snickered so loud she actually snorted. Then the nurse added: "Visit as long as you like and ask your guests to please stop by the front desk and say hello to me on their way out."

CHAPTER 7

History/Charlton Heston

Betty drew a deep breath, which rattled slightly in her chest, and then she began the story. "Well, Chief Smythe-Bates, I was born right here in glorious metropolitan Martin's Grove, New Mexico. That was a long time ago, back when dinosaurs roamed the earth. As I grew up, I became enamored with movie stars, like most of my friends. Back then, it was almost impossible to believe that the things and people we saw on the screen in a theater could be real. Imagine how Fred Astaire and Ginger Rogers looked to us, even in glorious black and white. When color films became common, it made things even worse, or better, depending on how you looked at it. I desperately wanted to see fabulous places and meet famous people. I didn't get to go as far as I'd hoped, but I went further than a lot of my friends...and I did it thanks to the movies. I got a job taking tickets at the Bijou Theater down on Third Street when I was a senior in high school. I eventually worked my way up to becoming the manager. Not exactly the big-time, but I saved enough for college. I earned my teaching degree and moved to Santa Fe. Definitely not Hollywood, but closer than Martin's Grove. I got a teaching job at South-Central-High School."

"Can I throw in my two-cents-worth?" Leonard Dunn asked. Betty nodded and Smythe-Bates shrugged his shoulders. "South-Central was the roughest high school in the roughest part of Santa Fe. Being a teacher there meant occasionally taking your own life in your hands," Dunn said, matter-of-factly."

"And you taught there?" the Police Chief asked. "Yes." Betty answered and smiled sincerely. Leonard interrupted again, this time without asking for permission. "She did more than teach there. There are a lot of people who would say that she saved that school *and* a bunch of the students who went there."

"That's amazing" chimed the Police Chief. Dunn when on: "That school had the highest failure rate and drop-out rate in the county until Miss Betty came along. She had a way of making you get your shit together." Betty replied: "I still do Leonard so please watch your language."

"Yes ma'am." Dunn answered with his head bowed slightly. I'm no statistician, but from what I recall, the first three years she was there, the drop-out rate was cut in half. She kept a lot of kids from quitting, including me." Police Chief asked her: "Would you be willing to share your secrets?" Betty perked up. "I used many tools my new British friend. I borrowed, umm, appropriated multiple clever catch-phrases from TV shows and commercials. Silly things such as: "Don't Be A Fool - Stay In School", or "Dropping Out? – So Will Your Paycheck". Sometimes all it took was the right ice-breaker to get their attention" The Police Chief asked: "Lenny, you said she was responsible for you getting into the fire-fighting business. How did that come to pass?"

"Well Eddie, that was a little more complicated." Chief Dunn answered. Betty gave him the kind of smile usually reserved for a loving parent to deliver to their child, and then she said: "Although it may also have started with the 'don't be a fool' line, I can't really say that I remember."

Dunn said: "Eddie, I decided I had to be a firefighter when Miss Betty told me the story of her hero. If you heard it, you'd understand." The Police Chief sat straight up in his chair. "This sounding considerably more interesting all the time. I'd love to hear it, if you wouldn't mind sharing it with me." Betty said: "Not at all. We've got permission to run past regular hours and just because it happened a long time ago doesn't make it a long story."

Miss Betty poured the remainder of her Gatorade into the tumbler on the bedside table, sipped it down and began her story: "I moved back to Martin's Grove for a while. Things had gotten really bad at South-Central high, just as Leonard described them." Her eyes welled up with tears as she said it. "The Board of Education was considering closing it down. I'd invested all the money I had in college and the move to Santa Fe. I was still a probationary teacher then and if they'd closed the school, I probably wouldn't have been offered another position. I didn't know what else to do. As much as I wanted to get away from here, all I could think of was to come back. Robert Frost said home is the place where, when you have to go there, they have to take you in. So, at thirty-eight I was back working at the Bijou again. Not as the manage but back to taking tickets, selling popcorn and candy, and sweeping the floors after every feature. I also stocked shelves at Cohen's clothing Store on Main Street downtown; that saved me some money. The owner let me stay for free in a rough but serviceable two-room apartment on the sixth floor over the store. He called it the penthouse because the building was only six stories tall. Somewhere around two A.M on March twenty-fifth in 1972, a light in a window display in the store caught fire while I was asleep in the *penthouse,* six stories up. I had no idea anything was happening until I heard sirens outside and caught sight of red lights flashing down on the street. But the most horrible thing of all, the thing I'll never forget if I live to be one hundred, which is getting shockingly close, was the smell. The smell of smoke was terrible. It was impossible to draw a breath without choking. I tried pulling the bed sheet up so a corner of it was over my nose and mouth but that just seemed to make it worse. I remembered hearing if you were trapped in a fire, get on the floor because the air stayed clearer down low. I got on the floor and crawled into the bathroom. I remember thinking of filling the tub with water and getting in it. But by then there was no water coming out of the faucets, I had no idea why.

It wasn't long before the smoke was getting so thick it was rolling under the door into the bathroom. Finally, I decided to make a run for the hallway and try to get downstairs. As I opened the door and ran through the smoke across the living room, a man's muffled voice shouted: "Stop!" I looked at the window that faced Main Street and saw a man looking in at me, six floors above the street below.

I was so scared I almost turned and ran back in the bathroom, completely confused from sheer panic.

But the man at the window put his hand up like a crossing guard telling a child to wait before crossing, and then he smiled at me. I stopped and stood still. For a few moments it was like time had stopped. Then he took an axe and broke the glass from the window and beckoned me to come toward him. I stumbled across the room, coughing and retching, nearly ready to pass out. When I got to the window, I saw he was at the top of a very tall ladder reaching up from a half-a-block long fire truck that was down at the curb. Just as I reached the window I fell to my knees. He reached in through the broken glass, grabbed me under my arms and lifted me outside. I was so happy to be able to draw a breath that I forgot I was six floors above the sidewalk, but only for a moment. When I turned my head in the direction of the concrete he said, "Don't look down." Then he threw me over his shoulders like I was a sack of laundry. I was going on forty years old then and not exactly a featherweight. And he did it at the top of a ladder six stories up.

I don't recall him backing down the ladder with me draped over his shoulders, but I do remember people on the street clapping and cheering when two other firemen lifted me from him at the bottom and set me on my feet beside the truck. I was coughing and wobbly, but before I'd even had a chance to blink the smoke from my eyes, the man who'd carried me to safety was standing beside me. He asked if I was okay. When I told him I'd be all right in a minute he smiled and said "That's wonderful." Then he handed me a little card and walked over to another lady sitting on the curb with a blanket wrapped around her shoulders. She looked like she felt every bit as rough as I did. He stayed with her for a few minutes before another firefighter came up and pulled him away for something. I took the opportunity to look at the card he'd given me. It was a very plain business card that simply said-**Phillip Stein/ Fire Chief, Martin's Grove, N.M.** That's how I met my hero. And a handsome hero he was. You remember me saying I was hooked on motion pictures?" Chief Smythe-Bates said: "Yes ma'am"

"Are you familiar with Charlton Heston?" The Police Chief nodded. "Yes, he was in Soylent Green wasn't he?" Betty held up her thumb. "Not to mention Ben Hur and the Ten Commandments. Well, I always thought Charlton Heston was <u>the</u> most handsome man ever born, until I saw Chief Stein's face in that window. He actually looked quite a bit like Charlton Heston, but Mr. Heston never pulled my ass out of a raging fire." Smythe-Bates grinned broadly. "Well, I can certainly see why he was your hero." Betty smiled at Leonard Dunn and said, "He's not the only one." Then she said: "Can you put up with me bending your ear just a little more?" The Police Chief said, "With pleasure."

"Well, you may have guessed they didn't close the school and I did eventually move back to Santa Fe. I eventually took on the guidance counselor duties and when the vice-principal retired, they convinced me to take the job."

Leonard Dunn spoke up: "That was the smartest thing that school board ever did! That's when that school stopped being a disgrace and became something to be proud of." He pointed at Betty. "And there's the reason, right there." Betty said, "That's where I met my other hero." She pointed at Dunn. Then she addressed the Police Chief. "Leonard was one of my success stories. He was headed in the wrong direction, but in the end, he made me very proud. He rescued me, when I needed rescuing." She paused and wiped her eyes with a tissue. "The board of education was decided to force me to retire at sixty-five, that was the mandatory retirement age. However, I didn't feel like I was quite ready to be put out to pasture." Smythe-Bates said: "Miss Betty, from what I've heard, you're as much a hero as anyone I've ever known. I've heard it said that a hero is someone who runs toward trouble instead of away from it. Taking on the kind of school you did, knowing what you were getting into, sounded pretty heroic to me. You do realize all heroes don't wear uniforms?"

"Yes, but some do." She smiled and again nodded toward Leonard Dunn. "Of course he didn't wear one then, but a petition was circulated around the school and to all the parents, lobbying to let me keep in my position. From what I hear, the person who started the whole project wasn't at all subtle about the proposal. He had no problem letting people know what he thought, thank God. When the petition was presented to the board, over fifty-five percent of the students had signed it, and every teacher and staff member except the man who'd got passed over when I took the vice-principal job. Can you guess who started the petition?" Now Betty was smiling, but real tears were streaming from her eyes. She added, "The board let me stay on until I was seventy-two."

Leonard Dunn walked over, put his arms around her shoulders and said: "I'm sorry Miss Betty, please don't cry."

Betty sniffed and wiped her eyes. "Don't worry Leonard, just like all heroes don't wear uniforms, all tears aren't bad." Then Betty looked at the Police Chief and said: "So you see, I've been rescued by Fire Chiefs twice. Is it so strange that I have a soft spot for men in uniform?" Dunn said: "After hearing how she was saved by a firefighter, I knew what I was supposed to do. I wasn't one of those kids who always knew what I wanted to be when I grew up; I had no plan at all. Before Miss Betty told me her story, I didn't know what I would do after graduation. I could have been in overalls hanging on the back of a garbage truck, but I saw an ad in the Martin's Grove Gazette that said the fire department needed recruits. I immediately thought if I didn't at least try it, I'd never forgive myself. You know, like what if that fire chief Stein hadn't been there for Miss Betty? So, I came here and applied, got the job, and I've been at it ever since." Betty said, somewhat reluctantly: "Well boys, it's time for me to take my meds and hit the sack. I've had a ball gabbing with you both and it wasn't just beating someone different at Jeopardy. It was just knowing that someone was listening to me like I'm someone useful, not like a flat tire that isn't worth the effort or cost of a patch. Oh, don't forget to stop at the desk on your way out."

"Yes ma'am, we will, and thank you for your gracious hospitality." Smythe-Bates gently took her wrinkled hand, being mindful of the gnarled appearance of her knuckles, and kissed it softly. Betty said: "Even without the hyphenated last name and the adorable accent I'd have known you were a foreigner." Smythe-Bates paused: "Oh, is that a fact?" Miss Betty turned up the corners of her mouth. "You're far too polite to be an American. Sadly, manners have fallen out of fashion in post-covid America. People got used to the idea that when half of your face is hidden behind a strip of paper or cloth, you could get away with anything. People stopped caring about simple things! Rude became the new national language." Betty stopped talking, put her head down, and drew a few ragged breaths, holding each one longer than the one before. Then she said, nearly in a whisper: "Sorry boys, I've got to take my dope and get some rack time."

Dunn made certain the nurse call button was within her reach, kissed her on the cheek, and said goodnight. Chief Smythe-Bates bent down and said: "Please forgive me being so forward ma'am." And he also planted a kiss on her cheek.

Betty said: "If I was only fifty years younger." Then her eyes drifted closed.

They stopped at the front desk and discovered the voice on the speaker had been that of Sandi VanMetre, the head nurse who had warned them of Miss Betty's prowess as a Jeopardy whiz. She was at a keyboard, tapping away when they arrived. She looked up at them and smiled but it was a half-hearted smile that didn't quite reach her eyes. It exhibited an almost equal mix of pleasure and sadness. Leonard said: "Hello, Miss VanMetre, isn't it?" The clerk nodded:

"Yes, but call me Sandi, please." Dunn continued: "Okay, Sandi it is. Miss Betty said you wanted to see us? Is there something we can do for you?" Sandi seemed not to know how to start. Dunn took the opportunity to ask a question: "Sandi, I was wondering, how is Miss Betty able to afford to stay here? This place doesn't seem very budget-friendly." Sandi frowned: "It's not. When word got around that Miss Betty needed help, the alumni association of the school got busy. The students ran a fund raiser and the Board of Education matched what they raised. There's enough money in a trust to keep her covered till she's a hundred and ten. I'd love to see her live that long. Now will you do something for me, if at all possible? Please, please promise me you will protect Miss Betty!" Dunn said: "With my life." Smythe-Bates jumped in: "That makes two of us. Tell me Sandi, what are we protecting her from?" She began to whisper conspiratorially: "There's a doctor here, Doctor French, a psychiatrist. He's out to get Miss Betty committed." Dunn's eyes flashed red and he said: "What! Where the hell is he? Point me to his office!"

Without thinking, Sandi glanced down the corridor that ran off to the left from the nurse's station. Dunn took three fast strides down the hall before Smythe-Bates caught up and grabbed him by the arm. "Lenny, Stop! I know how much you love this lady. I totally understand. I just met her and I feel quite the same. But I'm still the Police Chief and I can't let you potentially kill some bugger you know very little about. And because I'm the Police Chief, you can also be quite certain that I'll make sure no one railroads Miss Betty into anything dodgy. Now, let's calm down. I have no desire to lock up my new American friend, despite the fact that he's certifiably barmy. We still have a psycho fire-bug to catch." Leonard Dunn nodded as they walked back to the nurse's station. Dunn asked: "Now, Sandi, tell me what in the hell this is all about." Smythe-Bates added: "Forgive him, he gets emotional when it comes to Miss Betty." Sandi replied, "We all do. First off, I'll tell you why I personally care about her so much, if that's okay. Then I'll go from there." The Police Chief nodded "Please do." Sandi continued: "Fifteen months ago, my father died. My mother has been gone for over five years. I went into a spell of clinical depression and nothing has helped. Nothing! None of the standard treatments did shit. I had people recommend everything from sensory deprivation to acupuncture. I simply gave up. Of course Miss Betty noticed my mood, nothing gets past her. When she questioned me about it, I told her I felt so alone I no longer knew what I had to live for. You know what she said?" Leonard and Eddie spoke at the same time. "What?"

"She said, "Oh, the George Baily syndrome. You know what I think?" I said what?"

"George Baily syndrome is bullshit. It's a way to justify feeling sorry for yourself. Answer me two questions, all right?" I nodded and she said, "Have you had joy in your life?" I thought of when I saw my sister's newborn twins for the first time, and I nodded and said, "Yes." She said "Have you brought joy to others?" Immediately I thought of both of my parents cheering for me and crying at my nursing school graduation and I said, "Yes, of course." She said, "Then you've had a wonderful life. Now cut the crap and quit whining."

"Being talked to like a child apparently dragged me out of my depression as sure as a hook drags a fish out of a lake." Leonard Dunn said, a little impatiently, "So what's the story on this shrink?" Sandi got quieter"

"Well, he's a certified ass-hole. There's nothing clinical about that diagnosis, it's my opinion, pure and simple, though it's also the opinion of nearly everyone else who works here."

"He's published three books, and is highly thought of in the medical community. The only one around here who thinks highly of him is himself. I believe when he heard Miss Betty's story of the three-times Fire Chief Stein rescuing her, he started thinking of her as a chapter in a possible fourth book. It sure wasn't because he cared about her. I think he wants her in a place where he can get at her and study her any time he wants, like a fish in an aquarium." Chief Smythe-Bates looked confused. "Wait a minute: three times? She told us about him bringing her down from the burning building. What don't we know?" Sandi shuffled some papers and looked down the hall again. "That's the only thing she tells most people about, because it's undoubtedly true. The story was in the Martin's Grove Gazette back in '72. She was even quoted saying Chief Stein was more handsome than Charlton Heston. She knows if she mentioned the other two times to most people, she'd get a horse-laugh. She told me one evening when she was feeling blue and really needed someone to talk to, and I know I never told anybody. She must have told someone else who had loose lips. If I find out who I'll give em' a Reebok enema." Dunn said, "There's not a doubt in my mind."

Chief Smythe-Bates personally called and made an appointment for Leonard Dunn and himself to meet with Dr. French, the psychiatrist. He was afraid if Dunn intervened, they might *never* get to see the man, or that the doctor might pack up and leave the state. Doctor French's office was in the administrative wing of the building, far away from most of the resident's rooms. As they walked the hall toward his office, they passed a door with a sign over it that said Frank Hamilton, M.D. "Wonder what he does here," Dunn wondered aloud. The police chief rapped on the door. "I don't know Lenny, let us find out." A pleasant and unmistakably feminine voice answered: "Come in." Smythe-Bates opened the door and entered to find a woman in blue jeans and a white lab coat standing behind a desk polishing wire-framed glasses. She said: "Hello, may I help you?"

Smythe-Bates answered: "We were hoping to meet with Doctor Hamilton."

She stuck out her hand. "You have."

"Good day to you madam, I'm the Police Chief and you are a woman." the chief sputtered. "Wow," the woman said, smiling broadly. "Everything I've read about you is true; you really are an observational wizard." The Police Chief blushed slightly. "Please accept my most sincere apology. The sign at your door says Frank." The doctor pushed back in her chair. "It's a recent sign, made by a sign maker who will make no more signs for this establishment, I'm sure. It was supposed to say Fran, not Frank. Now, what can I do for you Chief?" Smythe-Bates slowed his respirations. "Well doctor, allow me to introduce the town's Fire Chief, Leonard Dunn." Dr. French stood up. "Okay, what can I do for you Chiefs, plural?" Dunn glanced at the Police Chief. "May I?" Dunn asked. Smythe-Bates nodded. Dunn asked, "First off, Doctor Hamilton, what kind of doctor are you? Are you a specialist?"

"Why do you ask?" she inquired, without hostility. "We're looking into what we believe may be a gross error in planned treatment for a patient who I know personally and happen to care a great deal about." Leonard Dunn answered, his voice becoming more strained as he spoke. The doctor relaxed and leaned back. "I'll answer your questions if you'll answer mine." Dunn nodded. "I'm a General Practitioner. It's my job to take care of the general health and welfare of our residents. Now, tell me who and what you are talking about." Smythe-Bates stepped into the conversation. "Are you familiar with Miss Betty Peacemaker?" She nodded. "And how about a Doctor French?" Again, she nodded. "I know them both. Betty Peacemaker is a sweetheart and Doctor French is an arrogant asshole whose absolute favorite person in the world is himself." The Police Chief let out a sigh. "Whew, I am happy we ran into you and I appreciate your candor. At least we have been forewarned. Otherwise, I might have had the unpleasant task of removing my friend's hands from around Dr. French's throat." "Please elaborate. What specific issue that has you so upset?" the doctor asked. Dunn answered: "We just found out this doctor that you called an asshole twice in the last ten minutes, wants to have Miss Betty committed.

With a severely disgusted look on her face, Doctor Hamilton said: "Of all the people in this place, including me, Miss Betty is the one who least needs or deserves to be committed." Smythe-Bates asked: "If it down came to brass tacks, would you be willing to recount that in a court of law?

Even if it might cost you your job?"

"Ask me a tough question." She smiled and nodded emphatically. "Okay, do you have any idea who she is especially close to in this facility, guests or staff who could give us more information?" She narrowed her eyes in thought and said: "Are you familiar with Nurse VanMetre?" Dunn grinned: "Yes ma'am, I was hoping you'd say her name."

The two chiefs walked back to the nurse's station. Leonard Dunn said: "Nurse VanMetre?" She reminded them: "Sandi, please." Chief Dunn continued: "Sandi, you mentioned two other times that Miss Betty said Fire Chief Stein rescued her two additional times, after he'd brought her down from the burning building." Sandi was resolute: "Yes!" Dunn wiggled his finger: "Please tell us more." Sandi stood and leaned on the fax machine: "Well, that event was well documented and indisputable. The other times were…uh…a little less cut-and dry. Miss Betty has been with us for going on three years. During that time, she's had two medical emergencies, both potentially life-threatening. On both occasions, I happened to be on duty and for that I'm grateful. Although I don't know if I made a damn bit of difference. If you listen to her explanation, she'd have been just fine without me being within a country-mile. I can't positively say that's she's not totally right." Sandi again paused, as if unsure how, or if to continue. "Please, go on, you're among friends." Dunn said. Sandi paused for a few seconds and caught her breath. "Okay. I hope you don't think I'm crazy. What sounds completely reasonable when Miss Betty tells it, sounds totally bat-shit senseless when I repeat it." After one more deep steady breath, Sandi recounted the story: "The guests usually go to the dining room to eat their meals. We want to keep them moving, but sometimes we'll slip an extra desert into a room later, for a special person, as long as it doesn't conflict with the diet on their chart. They don't come more special than Miss Betty.

One night an orderly slipped her a piece of apple pie. A fairly large piece of Granny Smith apparently went down the wrong pipe. She started to choke on it. Throat muscles aren't always as strong when you get up in years. She pushed the call button, and the alarms hooked to the electrodes plastered all over her were screaming. Miss Betty complained of a few chest pains and with her age, we knew she needed to be evaluated, ASAP. By the time I barged through the door, she was sitting up in bed, breathing perfectly. There was a good-sized, partially chewed piece of apple lying on the bedspread. When I asked her what happened, she just smiled and said, "I choked. But I'm okay. Captain Stein did that Heimlich thing. I examined her thoroughly and other than sounding a little bit hoarse, she appeared to be okay. But in less than ten minutes there were bruises coming up around her waist just below her ribs. Honest-to God." She paused and looked appraisingly at Chief Smythe-Bates. "You look more than a tad skeptical." The Police Chief smiled and said: "I can't really say. Tad is an American term. I'm not sure if I'm a bit skeptical or not. What I will say is coming from most people, I would refer to it as fantastical. However, you seem to be a quite serious and I judge you as quite credible." Nurse Sandi shuffled her feet and wrung her hands. "I try to be. But frankly, you ain't heard nothin' yet." "And I happen to have an EKG to back it up. We got a code-blue alarm from her room, patient in cardiac arrest. We went down the hall like a herd of horses. Before we could get there, the alarms had stopped. When we walked into the room, she was already pulling the electrodes off her chest, making a little ouch sound each time." She looked at me and said: "Calm down youngsters, Chief Stein gave me some CPR. May I please have another Gatorade?"….just like that. So, according to Miss Betty, her hero, Chief Stein, has saved her life three times now. Not just the one time that's been witnessed and well documented. That's why Doctor French wants to have her committed." Dunn, growled: "I thought in order for someone to be committed, it had to be proven that he or she is a danger to others or themselves." Sandi nodded. "That's true, but this ass-wipe is a master at finding loopholes. He'll keep kissing asses, bribing people and pulling in favors until he finds a judge who'll sign his commitment order." Leonard Dunn clinched his fists and yelled: "Over my dead body…or his!" Sandi said: "Chief Dunn, you and about fifty others I know feel the same way. Personally, if Miss Betty wants to believe in her own guardian-angel type hero, who am I to deny her that fantasy? All we can hope is that the old fossils on the review board man up and make Franks prove legitimate cause for his request. He'll have to get Doctor Hamilton and fifty percent of the senior nursing staff to sign off on it. I don't think there's a snowball's chance in hell of getting all those signatures. All he really wants is to put her somewhere that he can study her like a bug in a jar, any time he wants, for as long as he wants. I saw her chart. He's diagnosed her as suffering from a classic case of advanced Alzheimer's." Chief Smythe-Bates asked: "Does Doctor Hamilton concur with his diagnosis?" Sandi shook her head: "When she saw what he'd written on her chart she just rolled her eyes and mumbled something I didn't catch. I should say I didn't catch the words, but the tone was perfectly clear."

"I'm not a bit surprised, he answered. "I'm half Miss Betty's age and I'd kill to be as sharp as she is."

"That makes two of us", Sandi replied."

"Three," Dunn chimed in.. "So now what?" The Police Chief said: "Why don't you go to her room and just visit, Lenny? She clearly seems relaxed when you're around." Sandi agreed. "But don't mention anything about French to her. She doesn't need to worry about him." Chief Dunn gave a thumbs up. " I got this covered Sandi, and thanks for watching out for her."

"My pleasure," she answered sincerely. Then he asked Smythe-Bates: "What are you going to do?"The Police Chief headed towards the door. "I'm going back to the station, I still have a tip to follow up on." Dunn raised his left eyebrow. "So, you really have a tip? I thought that was something you said to cool off the nasty guy at the meeting." Smythe-Bates gestured with his hand. "No, I really do have a tip to chase. I don't know if it'll pan out, but I've got to chase it as far as I can and hope it turns into a substantial lead. This arsonist isn't likely to walk in my station with his hands on his head and surrender. You want to come along?" Dunn picked up his pace. "Absolutely: I'm not going to miss seeing an expert in action? "You know something Lenny? I never really know whether you're being serious or just being entertaining."

"Neither do I, Eddie." Both men laughed as they headed to their car.

In the police chief's office, Smythe-Bates opened a desk drawer and removed an old-fashioned Polaroid photo. He handed it to Dunn, who squinted at it and said. "What is it? It just looks like a blur to me." Yes indeed, at a glance it's hard to visualize , but it's actually an automobile." Chief Dunn replied. "In the good old USA, we prefer to call them cars. But okay, I'll humor you…what type of automobile is this? And where did you get this antique photo?" Smythe-Bates

shrugged his shoulders. "I bloody don't know what type of auto…er…I mean car this might be. I need a forensic laboratorist to figure this bugger out." It came with the tip I mentioned earlier. Jerome Akins, a concerned citizen who happened to be the chef at the second facility that burned, took it personally that the arsonist started the fire in his kitchen. So he put his old camera in his car and spent some time each evening cruising by the town's other nursing homes that might be targeted. He snapped this at the third home that burned. He said the car was just sitting outside idling so he snapped the picture. That night, the place burned to the ground. Dunn's interest was piqued. "Is this picture going to do you any good? You can't tell a thing about the "car" from that picture. Hell, I couldn't tell it was even a car until you told me." Smythe-Bates held up a finger and then pressed a button on his desk phone. A voice answered through the speaker: "Yes, Chief what do you need?" Presently, I need you in my office Johnson. Please come here for a moment."

"I'll be right there Chief. The door opened and a uniformed officer entered. He said: " What's up Chief?" Smythe-Bates told Dunn: "Officer Johnson is our department's car guy. He handed the photo to the officer. "Johnson, can you identify the make and model of that car?"

"Sorry Chief." Johnson said after studying the photo. There's just not enough detail." The Police Chief said "I've got an idea. Johnson, scan that into the computer and let me know when you've finished. I'll give you an e-mail address where to send it." Johnson snapped to attention. "Will do Skipper! What do you have in mind Chief?"

Smythe-Bates explained: The Yard has a database of all American automobiles. Their forensics team might be able to identify the make and model." Dunn seemed surprised. Scotland Yard has a database of American cars?" Smythe-Bates gave an explanation. "Yes Lenny, a lot of American cars are sold in the U.K. The manufacturers build them with right-side steering and pedals." "Holy shit" announced Dunn. The Police Chief continued. "That surprises you?" Johnson said: "I just always pictured the streets over there full of Rolls Royces and Bentleys." Smythe-Bates wrinkled his nose. "Do you see a lot of Rolls Royces and Bentleys over here?" Johnson shook his head. "Why do you think that is?" "Cause hardly anybody here can afford one?" Answered Johnson, timidly. The Police Chief went on. "Well, hardly anyone in U.K. can afford one either. That's why there are a lot of American cars in England and Scotland and Wales. Your assumption is a misconception perpetuated over the years by people who picked the idea up from Hollywood movies and watching the telly" He glanced at Dunn. "Similar I'm sure to the notion that police carry no guns, and every bloke loves warm beer, right Lenny."

"Yeah, very funny." Lenny's face flushed red as a ripe strawberry.

After a moment, the Chief's phone rang. He hit the speaker button and said, "Yes?" Johnson said, "The pic is scanned in. Give me the e-mail address and I'll get it on its way." The Chief gave him the address and said: "Put a note on it saying we need a make and model, as quickly as they can get it back to us."

"Aye aye Chief." Johnson felt like he was back in the Navy aboard the USS Carl Vinson, taking orders from his Division Officer. Chief Smythe-Bates picked up on Johnson's action. "Let me know ASAP when you get a reply." "Will do, sir!" Dunn asked: Eddie, what's next?"

"We wait." Smith-Bates surprised him by also saying, "Tom Petty said the waiting is the hardest part, and I agree." Dunn was shocked. "Wow Eddie, I didn't know you were a rock fan!"

"Lenny, I'm a very complicated and sophisticated man about town. But I don't consider myself to be a square." He glanced over his shoulder, laughing. Dunn was still in disbelief. "So, I'm discovering my Limey friend. I'm heading back to the fire station, call me if you find out anything about the mystery automobile." Smythe-Bates replied. "Very well. They're usually quite prompt. Scotland Yard has been around for a very long time; they are notably efficient.

Fifteen minutes later, Leonard Dunn's phone at the fire department rang. He recognized the number on caller ID as being a city hall extension. He answered with: "Did your big yard across the pond come through all ready?"

Smythe-Bates said: "That could have been an embarrassing interaction if it had been the mayor calling. Chief Dunn was unfazed. "I've been embarrassed before and survived. It wasn't the mayor, so I guessed right. Did you hear anything on the car?" The Police Chief was upbeat. Actually, yes. The computer identified it as a really old Ford Taurus, probably 1988 or 1989. They enhanced it enough to distinguish a color. Our mystery American automobile is a forest green 1988 or 89 Ford Taurus." Then he said: "Hold on, Mr. Johnson just slipped me a note. I told you he was our car guy. The note says, Chief, the Mercury Sable was the same car as the Taurus back then, just with a different badge. Like GM did with the Camaro and Firebird. Google says the Sable was also available in forest green. Scotland Yard's computer also spotted something else, the driver's side mirror was missing. So, Lenny, we're looking for an '88 or '89 Taurus or Sable in forest green and missing a mirror." Leonard seemed disappointed. "That's not much to go on, Eddie." The police chief replied: "It's more information than we had an hour ago old chap."

CHAPTER 8

The Shrink

By the time Chief Smythe-Bates managed to reach Doctor French's receptionist, word had made it through the grapevine that Leonard Dunn would be going into the meeting with him, primed for a fight. The receptionist said: "Doctor French made it clear that I'm not to arrange a meeting with Fire Chief Dunn unless you will also be present. Chief Smythe-Bates clarified: "Dr. French feels he may need police protection?"

"It certainly sounds like a possibility" the receptionist replied. "He was damn near sobbing." Chief Smythe-Bates said: "Unfortunately, I feel the same. My presence during the meeting probably is a wise decision. I actually haven't known Fire Chief Dunn for very long but it really doesn't appear it would take much to pull his pin. And once pulled, getting it back into the metaphorical grenade might be undoable. One thing in French's favor is Scotland Yard afforded me mandatory training in protecting subjects. For your knowledge, I've completed the course twice. Plus, I have some questions of my own for the fine doctor."

The following afternoon found both of the chiefs in Doctor French's waiting room. The Police Chief picked up a magazine from the stack on the table, flipped through it quickly and dropped it back onto the table. He lamented: "There is one thing apparently universal to doctor's waiting rooms, Lenny. Their magazine choices are at a minimum one year old." Dunn glanced at the magazine Smythe-Bates had skimmed through. "It may be old but a least it's Sports Illustrated and not something with Martha Stewart on the cover." After what seemed like forever, the receptionist stuck her head from her little glass window and said: "Doctor French will see you now, gentlemen." She pointed at the closed door and said: "Please knock before going in." Leonard Dunn bowed, replying: "I wouldn't have it any other way. Should I remove my shoes too, or do you think the doctor would read that as a latent maniacal tendency?"

"I assume you're Chief Dunn," she said.

Dunn quipped: "Yes, in the flesh."

"Well, you and your flesh are wasting your time and sarcasm on me. I just answer the phones and schedule appointments. I'd suggest using a different approach if you want to get anywhere with the doctor."

Smythe-Bates queried: "We've heard him referred to as an…" Before he could finish his sentence, the receptionist interrupted, "A shit-head?" Smythe-Bates chuckled: "Actually, the rather descriptive term we've heard was asshole."

She responded: "I work with him. I know him better than most, and I'd lean towards shit-head, although both apply. The best way to handle him is not let him bully you. He's one of those doctors who thinks his credentials make him superior to ordinary people. If you're here about what I think you're here about, I hope you kick his ass, metaphorically speaking, of course."

As it turned out, knocking on the door was not necessary. Just as the receptionist was completing her informative diatribe about the man, the door opened and Doctor French stepped into the waiting room. He immediately glared at the receptionist and growled: "Wanda, you should choose your words more wisely." Tapping on the door he'd just walked through, he said, "This door isn't exactly soundproof." He turned his attention to the two Chiefs. "May I assume you're here regarding Betty Peacemaker?" Chief Smythe-Bates answered through clenched teeth: "Indeed Dr French, you may assume that is the reason for our visit."

The doctor shook his head and said: "What is it about that woman that makes people soft in the head?" Dunn jumped into the conversation. "You've got it way wrong doc; she makes people soft in the heart." French asked, "How long have you known her?" Dunn shrugged: "At least a couple decades, how long have you known her?" The doctor crossed his arms and closed his eyes for a few seconds.

"Approximately three years. I've examined her at length and I feel I know what's best for her." Smythe-Bates said: "Doctor, with all due respect, and I haven't yet decided if *any* is due, we've just established that Chief Dunn has known Miss Betty far longer than you. I believe his opinion should be given fair consideration." Dunn nodded and added: "It would be a really wise idea on your part." French bristled: "That sounded like a threat Mr. Dunn." Doctor, that sounded like very strong recommendation. And please remember it's <u>CHIEF</u> DUNN!" Leonard Dunn was grinning from ear to ear. French said grudgingly: Come in to my office and we'll talk." The receptionist asked: "Is there anything else you need doctor?" Barking orders, Dr. French replied: "Yes: please call the head nurse and ask her to have Miss Peacemaker brought to my office immediately. In less than a minute, the receptionist reported back: "Nurse VanMetre says Miss Betty just sat down to lunch in the dining room. She'll try to have her here in ten or fifteen minutes." French looked disappointed. "Okay, go down the hall and tell Doctor Hamilton to be here by then too."

The two Chiefs were seated in Dr. French's office with Dr. Hamilton. The psychiatrist cracked his knuckles, releasing a deep sigh at the same time, making a display of the process. Dr. Hamilton pointed at the Fire and Police Chiefs and said: "For a change, there are a couple people sitting here who aren't a damned bit impressed by the diplomas on your wall. You're going to have to deal with someone who sees you for what you are." A few moments later, French's receptionist stuck her head in and said: "Nurse VanMetre and Miss Betty are here."

Franks made a sound that clearly indicated indignation, turned his back on her and said: "Show them in. Let's get this over with." The receptionist nodded and ducked out the door, but not before lifting a middle finger at the psychiatrist's back. The two Chiefs looked at each other and Dunn whispered: "I like her." Smythe-Bates kept a straight face but mouthed the words: "Me too".

When Sandi VanMetre and Miss Betty entered, Sandi quickly glanced at the few remaining empty chairs. She walked Miss Betty to the only empty padded chair in the room and eased her down into it. Dunn glared at French and said: "In case you aren't familiar with it, that's respect." Sandi chose for herself an armless, unpadded wooden chair. She sat down and assumed a posture that would make a Marine drill instructor proud, and folded her hands in her lap. Looking French straight in the eyes said: "What do *you* want?" The shrink said: "Ladies and gentlemen, we are here to address the matter of Betty Peacemaker, who is currently a resident of this facility." Sandi stopped him mid-sentence: "Knock off the Perry Mason crap, everyone knows why we're here."

"Including me." Miss Betty said. "You think I've got a screw loose, I'm half a bubble off plumb, not firing on all cylinders. My trolley is off the tracks, nutty as the proverbial fruitcake, one sandwich short of a picnic basket, one can short of a six-pack, or…I have bats in my belfry. Does that about cover it?" Everyone in the office laughed except for French, who clearly didn't see the humor in her brief dialogue. He growled: "I don't see the comedy in this situation." Leonard Dunn said: "Finally we agree on something, lucky for you." French looked at the Police Chief and said: "Are you going to let him continue to threaten me like that?" Smythe-Bates took a breath. "Dr. French, that is a difficult question for me to answer at this time. I promise to give it significant thought and consideration."

"Very funny," French curled his lip like an angry dog. "Do you want to hear what I have to say or not?" Sandi spoke up again: "Miss Betty, do you want to be here to listen to what he has to say? If not, I'll gladly take you back to your room." Betty's eyes were clear and bright: "No, I wouldn't miss this for the world. But please get on with it "doctor". I want to make sure I don't miss tonight's episode of Jeopardy."

"Okay." French started." "It's very simple. Miss Peacemaker has repeatedly presented with symptoms consistent with delusional behavior and is frequently disconnected from reality. Both are classic signs of advanced Alzheimer's"

"Says who?" Dunn said angrily. French cleared his throat. "It's obvious to a trained mental health professional. She can't tell what is real and what is fantasy. She is so fixated on the firefighter who saved her life a long time ago..."

"March twenty-fifth 1972 to be exact." Miss Betty interrupted. "The apartment was dark when I woke up to the sound of sirens so I couldn't see the clock or I'd tell you exactly what time. I'd guess it was about two am." French challenged her. "You actually can be that precise? After fifty years, you can recall the date and the details of the occurrence?"

"I'm no shrink, but that doesn't sound like Alzheimer's to me." The police chief said, his patience now wearing thin. French tapped on his desktop. "You're absolutely right about one thing, you're no psychiatrist. It's actually common for a person suffering with the disease to more clearly recall images and details of a situation their mind has processed than the actual memories. That way, their mind can adjust the memories to be more pleasant or have a more positive outcome." Chief Smythe-Bates asked. "So, you believe her other experiences were pure fiction?" French nodded. "I checked the city's records. Fire Chief Stein died while fighting a fire in 1980. Unless, of course, Miss Peacemaker, you believe you were saved not once, but twice by a ghost?"

Without a seconds' delay, Miss Betty said: "Not a ghost, a spirit. There's a difference you know."

"Is there really?" French asked, more amused than curious.

Yes, there's definitely a difference." Betty pressed on: "Actually it's very simple. Ghosts tend to be malicious or mean, spirits are just the opposite." French interrupted. "And what makes you so sure of that?" Betty answered: "Life experience, and my personal research." Please go on." French actually seemed anxious to hear her answer. "The life experience part is rather obvious. There's obviously nothing malevolent about saving me from choking or a heart attack. And research is easy, I might be old, but I can still read." Dr. French laughed.

"Oh, so you Googled…"what's the difference between a ghost and a spirit?"

Betty held up her arthritic hands, displaying twisted fingers and swollen knuckles. "No longer very keyboard friendly, but there are still ways." She licked the index and second finger of her right hand and pantomimed turning pages. French's tone became more sarcastic. Please enlighten us, what else have you researched?"

Betty glared at him. "I'll bet you didn't know that more translations of the Bible say Father, Son and Holy Spirit than Holy Ghost. I believe Don McClain only used ghost in 'American Pie' because it rhymed with most and coast. Also, Charles Dickens used spirit more than ghost in A Christmas Carol. The book, I mean. Not the movies that have made changes which mostly ruined the story. And Scrooge's visitors were certainly there to benefit him. Why do you think people say, "That's the spirit" as positive reinforcement, and not, "That's the ghost?" And when someone uses a negative to express doubt about succeeding, they say: "Not a ghost of a chance?" Dunn peered at Doctor French and said: "Alzheimer's huh?"

French took a parting shot: "So you think the spirit of the dead Fire Chief who saved you fifty years ago has become your guardian angel? He watches over you and protects you? Why would he specifically choose you?" Betty shrugged: "Not an angel, a spirit. I'm only telling what he's done. I couldn't begin to say why he has done it for me. I can only guess…and guessing is for people with a lot of diplomas on their office walls." Dunn laughed aloud. French stood abruptly and shouted: "Miss Peacemaker, I'm tired of talking to you." Betty snapped back:

"Not as tired as I am of hearing you talk!" Sandi VanMetre stood and said: "Come on Miss Betty, let's get you back to your room. You're looking a bit tired. We'll stop by the desk and get you a Gatorade." Betty winked. "Still no Bud Light?"

Sandi replied: "I'm afraid not." As Sandi and Miss Betty walked out the door, Betty looked over her shoulder at Doctor French and said: "Alzheimer's my ass!"

On the way back to her room Sandi said, "Don't worry about him Miss Betty, that man has an ego the size of Montana, and a mind as narrow as a supermodel's waist. You've got a lot of people on your side, looking out for you." "Yes, I've been very fortunate as far as being looked out for," she answered with a small satisfied smile.

C H A P T E R   9

The Mystery Car

As they were leaving the nursing home, the Fire Chief asked the Police Chief: "Well Chief Inspector Clouseau, what's are next move?" Smythe-Bates was amused: "My dear American friend, you have chosen to compare me to a fictional character from France. You do remember that I'm a British subject.

I am promptly going to my office and follow up on the tip I got from the Yard's intel division. Do you care to come along?" Dunn got serious, "Sure do, I'm not going to miss a chance to see you in action. I've got to go by the fire station and make sure things are okay, then I'll be right over." When Dunn arrived at the Police Chief's office, Smythe-Bates said: Here it is and handed him a blurry, out-of-focus photo. Chief Dunn grabbed the photo. "What's this, it just looks like another big dark blob to me." Smythe-Bates agreed. "Yes, but sadly, that is the best lead we have so far. Dunn pushed for more info. "That's sad. What is it? Can *you* tell? Who even took this picture?" Police Chief Smythe-Bates elaborated. It is most likely an automobile and the picture was shot in the evening under poorest lighting conditions. A concerned citizen named Jerome Akins, he was a sous chef at the second nursing home and he took it personally that the fire-bug started the blaze in his kitchen. He took it on himself to take his camera and spend his evenings driving around to the other nursing homes and watching for the culprit. He spotted this car sitting in the employee lot of the third nursing home. The place was torched that night. He said he tried to get a picture of the license plate, but the car was behind another car and he couldn't get close enough to see it or write it down.

"So, does this help at all?" asked Dunn. "Maybe." The Chief pushed the button on the intercom.

When the dispatcher out front answered he said: "Please ask Johnson to come to my office again. In a few moments a knock came at the door. The Chief said, "Come on in Mr. Johnson." The uniformed patrol officer came in and the Chief reintroduced him to Dunn. "Remember Officer Johnson, our car-guy? I'm hoping he can shed some specks light on this situation." He handed the blurry underexposed photo to Johnson and asked: "Do you have a clue this one? After examining the picture closely, Johnson said: "Sorry chief, I can't see anything that I recognize as a particular make or model." Johnson, please scan that picture in and send it to the address I gave you earlier. Include a note from me about what we need and…use ASAP in the subject line, again." The chief's intercom buzzed and Johnson said, "The photo is winging its way across the pond, Chief." Unless you want me to hang around, I'm going to the fire station and check in. Call me if you hear anything on the mystery car." "I will, right away." Dunn left for the firehouse.

Fifteen minutes later Smythe-Bates called him and said: "Johnson just got another answer from The Yard." Dunn could feel his heart race. "I'll be there in five minutes." Smythe-Bates said calmly: "Be careful, I'm much too busy to write a speeding ticket to a colleague." When the two chiefs were in Smythe-Bates' office, he buzzed Johnson and told him they were ready. Johnson came in and gave his report. "Their forensics computer ID'd the car as a late 80s Ford Taurus. Pic enhancement say forest green again. But don't forget my previous observation that Ford also made the Mercury Sable. Same exact car, different badge. Their computer also spotted the missing a driver's side mirror.

The Police Chief tried to stay calm: "This is quite interesting. I'm trying with great difficulty to not get overly excited."

Dunn said: "Not an impossible task, we just have to find a guy who has a bad right ankle. drives a forest green late 1980s Taurus or Sable with a missing mirror, and wears size 10 Nikes with a tack in the sole of the right one. Sounds like a piece of cake." The Police Chief lifted one eyebrow again. "If Miss Betty were here, she'd be rather disappointed that you didn't say That's the Spirit!"

Chief Dunn rubbed his forehead: "You're right, these leads seem to be heading us down a logical pathway. What do we do now?" Smythe-Bates asked: "I'm new here, obviously. In the UK, all registered vehicles have a data point related to color of the exterior. Do you know if New Mexico tracks the color of vehicles they register?" Dunn said: "I'm not sure, but it shouldn't be too hard to find out."

Chief Smythe-Bates stretched back in his chair. "I'll get Johnson on it right away. In the meantime, I'm going to try something that might be labeled a long-shot, but I believe it is certainly worth a try." He picked up the phone and buzzed Johnson, asked him to check with the DMV about tracking auto colors, and then said:

"Please find me the number for that very large Ford dealership just outside of town." They heard the clicking of a keyboard from Johnson's end, and the officer read off a phone number. The Chief jotted it down and dialed it. When the Ford dealer answered, he asked for the parts department and asked the clerk who picked up the phone to check if he'd had any orders for a driver's side mirror for a late 80s Taurus or Sable in forest green.

He heard more keyboard clicking, then the man said: "I don't have any outstanding orders, but you might try the body shops in the area. A lot of people go to them for older parts. They have a network to locate second-hand parts for the older models. He thanked the man and buzzed officer Johnson again, told him to round up names and numbers for area body shops. Johnson brought him a list of five in less than a minute. He also said he'd found out that the DMV did not record colors for the cars they registered. The Chief started down the list of body shops, asking each he called if they had anybody call about the mirror. He got lucky with the third shop. The man said, "I can do better than that. Give me a couple minutes to check my files and I'll give you the name and address of a dude who bought one off of me over a month and a half ago."

The body shop owner produced the receipt and read it to him, the Chief scribbled down the information. "The car parts guy added, "He was kind of creepy, I didn't like him right off, and I like most people." The Police Chief asked: "What didn't you like about him?"

Car parts guy opened up: "He was kind of weaselly and sneered toward the door and rolled his eyes when an elderly black couple came in looking for a part for their grandson." The Chief thanked him and hung up.

He looked at Dunn: "Bingo! This absolutely lovely! That man sold a forest green driver's side mirror one month ago. I have the buyers name and address. Chief read it aloud: "Raymond Bruce. Does that ring any bells with you?"

"No, sorry." Said Dunn. "A month and a half? That picture was taken just a few weeks ago." Chief Smythe-Bates replied: "I am aware, but all we can do is hope that if this our fire-bug, he's simply been too busy to put the replacement mirror on between the most recent nursing home fires. Even if he puts it on before we apprehend him, it will be strikingly obvious it's been replaced." So, my Yankee Doodle fire fighter, now we wait." Chief Dunn said: "I know how much you and Tom Petty hate waiting."

Smythe-Bates got on the phone to the state police and asked if they had any information on Raymond Bruce. They promised a call as soon as they ran his name through all the criminal databases. The call came in 30 minutes and it told them nothing. The State trooper said: "Just because we have nothing on your guy doesn't mean he doesn't have a history. If he committed a misdemeanor that was investigated locally, we wouldn't necessarily have info on it. Check with your county's Sheriff or local constables. You just might get lucky there."

The police chief repeated his call, this time to the Sheriff. After listening to some Olympic speed typing from the woman on the other end of the call, suddenly she spoke: "Chief, your boy has a record. He moved to our area from Nogales, Arizona. When the sheriff there found out where he was headed, he gave us a call to warn us to watch him." Smythe-Bates became curious: "What offenses did he do in Arizona?"

The Sherrif's clerk replied: "He was charged with cruelty to animals and arson, both on the same charging document. He was teasing a neighbor's dog and got bitten.

That night somebody poured gas on the dog house and lit it while the dog was in it. The homeowner saw the flames and used an extinguisher. The dog was burned, but survived. The homeowner saw someone running away and took a shot him with a 12-gauge shotgun, but unfortunately missed. Bruce produced one of his good-old-boy friends who provided an alibi, so he got off. No one in town would have anything to do with him after that incident. Everybody knew the dog's owner, and the dog.

Bruce got fired from his gas station job and nobody else would hire him. He packed up and left town in the middle of the night. The only way the sheriff knew where he went was by checking with the post office. Bruce had filled out a change-of address form showing Martin's Grove general delivery as his new mailing address. That's what we know. Does that help you?" Chief Smythe-Bates was almost laughing. "More than you'd believe.

Thank you!" The clerk sensed his excitement. "I hope you get him."

"We will, replied the Police Chief. Goodbye and thank you again."

The clerk flirted a little: "You're very welcome, and…I love your accent."

CHAPTER 10

Foxhole

The next day when morning visiting hours began, the two Chiefs were waiting outside room 108. Chief Dunn knocked and Miss Betty said in her usual energetic voice: "Come on in, whoever it is, I'm bored to death!" When they were seated, the Police Chief asked: "How are you, Miss Betty?"

"I've been better," she said with a tiny, bent smile, "but I've also been a lot worse. I can't find a thing to watch." She pointed at the TV mounted on the wall. "It seems like all you can find in the morning are ancient game shows or the repetitive news, and all they talk about is that fool still claiming he won the election." Now she scowling. Then she asked: "What are you two fine fellows up to this crisp New Mexico morning?" Dunn said: "We just wanted to visit the smartest and most interesting person on the planet." Miss Betty winked at Dunn. 'Too late, Alex Trebek died last year." Smythe-Bates said: "It's a shame they didn't hold open auditions for a new host Miss Betty! Had that happened, you would be in Hollywood hosting the show, I probably would be in London, fishing in the River Thames." Betty smiled:

I'm sure you would have found the strength to survive." Then she said: "If you boys would take a brief stroll down the hall to the waiting room, I have left something undone this morning."

"Dunn said: "Yes ma'am, some things simply can't wait." With a smile Betty said, "It's not that, I simply haven't said my morning prayers." The Police Chief answered: "Yes ma'am, we will step out." Then he added: "With everything you have had to deal with, you still pray? I imagine almost dying in the fire, choking to almost near death, and a heart attack?"

"Did you ever hear the saying; there are no atheists in a foxhole?" The Chief nodded. "Well Chief Smythe-Bates, he of good manners and fetching accent, I've been in a foxhole since I woke up smelling smoke in that *penthouse,* fifty years ago. Then, almost choking to death and a heart attack kept me there. I even managed to make my husband see the light."

"Husband!" Dunn said. "You were married?" Betty nodded. "Yes, but not nearly long enough. When I was still in Santa Fe, I met a wonderful man named Jonathan. He was the custodian at the school. We fell in love and were married. Our marriage was wonderful while it lasted, but less than four months after saying our vows, he dropped over with a heart attack. He lingered for the next eight hours. Everybody knew me by Betty Peacemaker, they hadn't even gotten me a new nameplate for my desk in the school office yet. So, I decided to be Betty Peacemaker again. But not long before he died, I believe I changed his mind. He'd been an atheist all his life, but I told him if there weren't a God I'd have died in that fire years ago. Surprisingly, he told me he would give up being an atheist for Lent. He said it as a joke but he actually went to the Sunday service with me, and a light went on for him during the homily. Then he was gone and my foxhole got even deeper. But I know he gained a belief in Heaven in the short time we had. I had a moment to say goodbye to Jonathan in the hospital. Just before his eyes closed, he said, see you later Babe."

When the two Chiefs returned from their brief walk after giving Betty her privacy, she asked them: "Tell me, are you two having any success on your quest to collar the fire-bug?" The Police Chief said: "It looks like there might be a light at the end of the tunnel." Betty squeezed their hands: "I'm happy to hear boys, as long as it doesn't turn out to be an oncoming locomotive."

CHAPTER 11

Raymond Bruce

When the two Chiefs left Care-Haven Acres, it was raining cats-and-dogs. Chief Smythe-Bates said: "Lenny, why in the world did you park so far away?" pointing at the big red SUV parked at the far end of the lot. Dunn said, "Believe it or not, there is a method to my madness. I thought that if our guy happened to drive by and saw what amounted to a bright red sea of Fire & Rescue vehicles near the entrance, it might make him do one of two things. It might scare him into pulling up stakes and hitting the road, or he might decide that times-a-wasting and get impatient. Hopefully, if he does get in a hurry, then he'll get sloppy or careless and tip his hand. At least know what kind of car he drives." "Assuming Raymond Bruce is our perpetrator." the Police Chief answered. "There are probably more than one forest green Ford Taurus in this part of New Mexico." Chief Dunn nodded. "Yeah, but not many of them will belong to a perp with a history like his. I mean he did try to cook a dog in its dog house. Isn't that what you lawmen call a clue?" Smythe-Bates thought for a moment. "Actually, rather than clue, I like to think it is this chap's profile. Lenny, what are you trying to do, take my job?"

"No way Eddie, I've seen the black and white car they assigned you, it's very unimpressive."

"So, you took the job for the red SUV?" grinning at Dunn. "I thought you were the personification of the unselfish public servant." The fire chief nodded at the SUV across the lot and said: "Eddie, that monster gets five miles per gallon and I'm only allowed so many miles per month on the city's dime. After that, I owe for the gas I use," He paused: "I mean the *petrol* I use comes out of my pitifully under-stuffed wallet. This unselfish public servant would be better off financially if Martin's Grove provided me with a bright red Honda Civic. But I'll tell you what: you stay here, I'll go get soaked and pick you up." Then after a dramatic pause he said: "Hey I thought you'd be used to getting rained on, being from England." Smythe-Bates countered: "It doesn't *always* rain there."

Covering his head and running towards his SUV, Dunn laughed: "Yeah, and cops do carry guns and drink their beer cold. I'm going to have to quit watching BBC America."

After leaving Care-Haven Acres, the Fire Chief turned left, taking them out of town instead of right, toward the fire and police stations. "Where are we going Lenny?" asked a puzzled Symthe-Bates. Dunn looked straight ahead. "Eddie, I thought while I have you with me, we might do a little detective work. Did you check the address the parts guy gave you for Raymond Bruce?" The Police Chief nodded: "I sent Johnson out to the address. It was an overgrown lot with a rusty, rat-infested looking mobile home. He knocked but got no response. He also walked the entire property looking for a sign of the Taurus or Sable. Unfortunately, no luck. I'm going to put an officer near the property in case Bruce shows up. There is a high probability that this individual fled to avoid capture." Dunn snickered. "What is so bloody funny?" Dunn reigned in his laughter. "I was just wondering how many years it's been since I heard anyone use the word <u>fled</u>."

The Police Chief frowned: "Lenny, I know that word is used in the States. I've heard it on an episode of Law-And-Order, a very popular show on the Telly in the UK. We clearly are two nations divided by a common language." Dunn replied:

"So, you don't want to ride by the place?" Smythe-Bates leaned forward and peered through the windshield. The wipers were having a hard time keeping up with the driving rain. He said: "I'm not opposed, and we're obviously soaked to the skin. If we don't see any signs of life, we won't get out." "Sounds like a plan Dick Tracy."

Dunn concentrated on guiding the big vehicle through the downpour. In just over over five minutes, he pulled up beside a rusty mailbox on a badly rotted post. A crooked gravel lane trailed off into a forest of weeds. "This is the place." Dunn declared. He reached in the glove box and fished out his binoculars. Handing them to the Police Chief, he said: "I'll ease up the driveway, you keep a watch up ahead. If he's here, the rain might keep him from seeing or hearing us coming. As they approached the mobile home, Dunn stopped the vehicle and stepped out in the rain. Before closing the door, he said, "Give me the binoculars, Eddie. I want to look around without having to see through the windshield." Smythe-Bates handed them over after scanning the property and said: "No Taurus or Sable, but I can see some relatively deep tire tracks that haven't filled with water yet. The tracks aren't wide enough to be from a truck or SUV. They must have been left by pretty big auto and I'd surmise it was here not too long before the rain." Dunn agreed: "Eddie, a Taurus is a big car, maybe we're on the right track." Smythe-Bates looked disappointed. "Yes, but I truly wish we'd found the bastard here." Dunn asked: "So now what? Do you want to wait?" The Police Chief shook his head. "Get back in and drive up to the mobile home, I want to check on something else."

"You got it." Dunn pulled the SUV up to the front door of the decrepit trailer, and then said: "Now what?" Smythe-Bates yelled: "Lenny, I think I smell smoke, don't you." He winked. "I sure as hell do, Eddie. It's justification for a health and welfare check, just to assess the well-being of anyone who might be inside, of course." They climbed out and walked to the door. The Police Chief pounded on it but heard nothing from inside. He tried the knob, with no results. Dunn held up his arms: "Now what?" Smythe-Bates pointed at the door. "Now we do the right thing Lenny, we follow the smoke smell. It is clearly as plain as the nose on your face." Dunn lifted his head and sniffed, then winked. "Damn, you're right. It's getting stronger all the time! If there's one thing I recognize, it's the smell of smoke." Then he said, "You or me?" Smythe-Bates answered: "I recall you calling me spindly earlier on, I'll classify you as the bulky one. Please, be my guest." He drew his gun and stepped aside.

Leonard Dunn backed up a little and shifted from one foot to the other a few times to get his balance. Then he looked at the Police Chief and said: '"On three," and got a nod in return. Smythe-Bates stepped up beside him and counted: "One, Two, Three, go, go, go!" Dunn stepped forward and kicked the door right beside the knob. There was a crash as the door lock shattered, and it swung open with a squalling noise from the rusty hinges. Smythe-Bates stepped in front of Dunn and pointed his gun into the shadowy interior. After a moment he asked: "Do you hear anything?" Dunn said: "No, but that smoke smell is getting stronger." He chuckled and asked: "Does that qualify as probable cause?" The Police Chief shook his head. "No, but I really want this bastard. If there's a problem with us breaking & entering, they can send me back to London, but hopefully not until we nail this guy." They moved farther into the dark mobile home. The drapes were drawn, presumably to keep out prying eyes. Dunn said: "I forgot my flashlight in the SUV, you want me to get it?"

"No, I've got a torch." The Police Chief pulled a lighter from his pocket and flicked it alight. "I didn't know you're a smoker, Eddie. I've never seen you do it."

"I don't smoke anymore, fortunately broke that habit but I can't break the habit of putting the lighter in my pocket. Let's try that way." He pointed down a hallway. Smythe-Bates led the way, his lighter held out before him. They passed a bathroom and a sliding door that opened on a closet. A few more steps, they came to a locked door. Dunn said, "Same plan as the front door?"

"No, Lenny: this one's on me." He grabbed the knob and slammed his shoulder against the door. The whole trailer trembled but the door didn't open. A second try split the door in two. "Damn, Eddie! Not bad for a spindly cop. Maybe I misjudged you." Behind the door was a bedroom. It was as dark as the rest of the place. The lighter showed that in the far wall was a door, secured with a hasp and padlock.

Smythe-Bates said: "Looks like Mr. Bruce has something he wants to keep a secret."

Dunn stepped in front: "Yeah, let me see if I can find a way to fix this problem. Let me have your lighter. I'll look for a key." Dunn took the lighter and followed its meager light until he found the kitchen. He came back into the bedroom. "I found a key Eddie." He held up a shiny red fire extinguisher. "I think it'll fit the lock. He gave the Police Chief his lighter and lifted the extinguisher with both hands and brought it down on the padlock. The lock and hasp ripped from the wood and flew across the room.

Smythe-Bates said: "You were correct in your assumption Lenny, it did indeed fit. Kind of appropriate I say, unlocking an arsonist's door with an extinguisher." Dunn pulled the door open and found a large closet. He crouched down and peered into its dark interior. The Police Chief asked: "Do you want the lighter?" Dunn backed up. "No, definitely not! I can't see much, but I see enough to know a lighter is *not* a good idea."

Smythe-Bates walked to the closest window and ripped the curtains down. The light from the window was dim and uneven, as rain water trickled down glass.

But it was enough and Dunn immediately said: "I'm glad you didn't use that lighter!" He stood up, holding a gasoline can in each hand, both cans making a sloshing sound. "Holy shit!" Dunn was cracking up with laughter. "You know what, Eddie? "Your accent is barely noticeable when you're scared out of your mind." Duly noted said the Police Chief. "Then I'm sure you're not picking up on it now. Would there be petrol in those receptacles?" Dunn shook the cans a little. "This one's almost empty, the other feels about half full."

Then he asked: "Do you think this makes it more likely Raymond Bruce is our guy?" Chief Smythe-Bates concurred. "I'd say it does. Where I come from people don't keep cans of petrol in their bedroom closet. I'd also say he has a special reason for doing so. Let's check this entire cesspool and see what else turns up."

Chief Dunn said: "Absolutely", and then he spoke up: "Hey wait! Lookie here!" Dunn took hold of the edge of the closet's back wall and pulled. With a creak, the bottom half swung open like a door. "Mister Bruce definitely has a secret." He reached in the now-exposed space and dragged out a small suitcase.

Dunn asked: "Should we open it?" Smythe-Bates replied: "We've broken just about every rule regarding search and seizure and chain-of-custody, why stop now? Give it to me Lenny." Dunn asked. "What are you going to do?"

Smythe-Bates explained: "I'm going outside and see exactly how far I can throw this grip. If it doesn't explode or burst into flames once it lands, we'll assume it wasn't rigged." Dunn turned his head: "What will that tell us Eddie?"

"That he's not scared of us enough to set booby-traps. The front door didn't explode when you kicked it in. He probably thinks he's still unidentified as a suspect. That could be a good thing. He could get careless if he thinks he's not being watched. Dunn said, "That wouldn't be my first choice, but it's the only plan we've got. Just make sure you give it one hell of a heave. I don't want to catch any shrapnel." Smythe-Bates picked up the suitcase and walked to the door. Once outside, he began swinging the case back and forth in an underhand arc.

After a few swings he said: "Fire in the hole!" and let the suitcase go. It flew thirty feet and landed with a thud. Nothing happened but a clod of mud and brown grass flying up in the air. Smythe-Bates said: "I just love it when a plan comes together."

They walked to where the suitcase landed. Dunn bent down and looked it over. "Here goes!" He flipped the pair if latches and lifted the cover. "Wow. It's too late to give us probable cause for breaking in, but it's interesting." Inside laid three small boxes about ten inches square. On each was an illustration and description of the contents: Compact wind-up travel alarm clock. "Bingo!" the Police Chief exclaimed. "Now we know he is our guy." Dunn reminded Eddie: "We still don't know where he's hiding out."

"We'll find him, Lenny, and look there." He pointed at a small zip-up bag. In it were several inch-long pieces of electrical wire.

"Those my friend are igniters. They are used to light the engines of model rockets. When a small electrical charge goes through them, they heat up like the filament in a torch bulb.

In this guy's case, he uses them to start fires. He probably covers them with something like paper or sawdust. The alarm clock closes the switch, the igniter heats up and starts the fire." Dunn said: "So now, beyond a shadow of a doubt, Raymond Bruce is our guy? Smythe-Bates smiled: "Without the slightest doubt. I'll put out an all-points-bulletin for him and the car and we'll keep a close watch on Care-Haven-Acres, day and night. Hopefully, if he does try something, we'll collar him before he can pull it off." Dunn looked at his watch. "I have to get back to the fire station. Are you about ready to go?" Chief Smythe-Bates said: "Just five more minutes, please. Let's perform one more sweep of this dumpster on wheels. Maybe we'll find a further clue about where he's gone.""

They again entered the mobile home and started searching. With the rain now stopped, they had sufficient light by opening all the curtains. In the bedroom where they had found the closet full of evidence, Smythe-Bates bent over and looked under the bed. The Police Chief reached under and pulled out a pair of dirty sneakers. He looked over the Nikes, labeled size 10. Flipped the right one over and looked at the sole. Chief Dunn looked over his shoulder at the shoe and said: "I'm impressed…uneven sole wear and a nail in it. Is that where most serial arsonists put their shoes?"

"I don't know." Answered the Police Chief. "But it's where I put mine. I had a hunch they would be there and that turned out to be correct." Dunn was happy. "Well, we didn't find our perp, but finding his shoes are more proof that he did it; more evidence if we get him in a courtroom," Smythe-Bates said, "Not *if*, but *when* we get him into a courtroom." The Fire

Chief said: "Eddie, it'll be getting dark soon, so if it's okay, I'll drop you off at your office. Then I'm going to the fire station and see if things are okay there, I've been out more than in lately. Let me know if the A.P.B. produces anything results."

"Indeed Mr. Leonard, things are coalescing brilliantly. I will contact your cell number if when receive updated information."

At 8:30 pm, Leonard Dunn's cell phone rang as he was pulling away from the McDonalds Drive-through. He recognized the number and answered: "What's up Eddie? I just picked up dinner from Mickey-D's. If I don't get Monica's Big Mac to her while it's still hot, there'll be hell to pay." Smythe-Bates tone was short. "You'll have to microwave it later. I'm at the station and I just got a call from Jerome Akins, the chef who snapped the picture of the suspect's car. He was out doing errands and drove past Care-Haven-Acres. He says the forest green mystery car is sitting in the back parking lot with the engine running." Dunn said: "I'll be at the police station in five minutes!" I'll be ready!" Smythe- Bates yelled into the phone and strapped on his big revolver. Dunn threw the McDonalds bag over his shoulder into the back seat and hit the gas pedal.

Twelve minutes later, Leonard Dunn's fire-engine-red SUV slid around the turn into the driveway of Care-Haven Acres. The bubble-light on top was spinning, throwing strobe-like flashes of blinding bright red light in all directions. He'd had the siren on until they were less than a mile from the facility. Then Smythe-Bates recommended he turn it off to avoid notifying Raymond Bruce that they were coming. The automatic gate slid open and they sped through. Dunn jerked the wheel and steered toward the end of the L-shaped building, skirting the edge of the property, and soon they could see the back parking lot. Across the lot, the forest green Ford sat near the foot of a short set of concrete steps that led up to the emergency exit door they'd seen on their inspection trip. Exhaust vapor plumed from its tailpipe, looking like a white cloud in the moonlight. Dunn hit the gas and the big vehicle accelerated across the lot straight toward the idling car. Over the roar of the engine, they heard a yelping siren from the building. Smythe-Bates yelled: "Lenny, what in the hell are you doing?"

"I'm making sure that if he slips by us, he doesn't go anywhere in that car." The big SUV closed the distance in seconds and collided with the right-front fender of the Taurus. There was a huge crashing sound and the car spun around like it was on a turntable, with both tires on the right side flat and practically torn from the wheels. With both hands planted on the dashboard the Police Chief said: "Very well done, mission accomplished! That car's going nowhere." Then he shouted: "What in the hell!" and pointed at the door. As they watched, the door flew open and a figure burst through, took a clumsy out-of-control stride and toppled forward down the steps to the sidewalk that led up to them. Then a brilliant flash of fire erupted where the figure had fallen. Both of the Chiefs were blinded by the flash of flames that flew out in all directions. Dunn screamed: "Jesus and Mary, what was that?" The Police Chief was shocked. "I don't know Lennie, you're the fire expert in this vehicle!"

At the foot of the steps, they found the body of a man. In the yellowish glow of a light that hung on the wall over the door, they could see the body was burnt beyond recognition. Dunn asked: "Is that Raymond Bruce?" Smythe-Bates responded:

"Damned if I know. It will probably require dental records to positively I.D. this mess."

CHAPTER 12

Miss Betty

A moment before fire chief Dunn's SUV slammed into the old Ford Taurus, sending it spinning like a top, Miss Betty opened her eyes. For a scary moment she thought she'd gone back in time, half a century. She lifted her head like a dog catching a scent and fighting the urge to hold her breath, sniffed the air and caught a smell she'd prayed for fifty years to never smell again. The air was filled with the odor of smoke. She snapped on the light over her bed and saw a cloud of gray smoke clinging to the ceiling. Swinging her legs off the bed, she got to her feet and stumbled to the door. She pressed her ear to the door, expecting to hear the sound of running feet, but the hall was silent. She glanced at the bedside phone, but decided against it. If she pressed the button for the nurse's station, whoever answered would spend at least a minute scolding her for not being in bed before she could squeeze in a word to warn them of a fire. After drawing a breath that made her cough, she twisted the knob and opened the door.

Before stepping into the hall, she glanced back at the window and made a wish; to not be back in the *Penthouse* a long time ago but to see Fire Chief Stein looking in, ready to save her. All she saw was darkness. When the door opened, she did hear the sound of running feet. Not the pounding of a hundred feet, but the slap-slap of a just a person or two running toward her from the direction of the kitchen. She squeezed her eyes shut and opened them again, trying to blink away the smoke-sting. Then she stepped into the hall. It was dimly lit by the murky glow of an emergency light that had come on two doors away from her room. Betty turned toward the oncoming sound of the running feet and squinted in the smoky semi-darkness. Two figures became visible, coming toward her fast, one directly behind the other. When they were close enough to her that they came into the circle of illumination from the emergency light. It became obvious the figure in front was running as hard as possible to put distance between himself and the other. She could hear the labored sound of the man gasping for breath. When he was close enough for her to see his face, she peered at him, expecting to see a familiar staff member, or possibly another guest, but he was a total stranger to her. The one thing she knew immediately was that the strange man was terrified. She'd never seen a person look so scared. His arms were pumping like a runner heading for a finish line, and she heard an odd repetitive thumping that sounded in time with his movement. Then she saw the man was carrying a red-painted can that was bouncing off his right knee with every stride. When the two figures had closed the distance sufficiently for her to see the man chasing the frightened stranger, her heart skipped a beat and leapt for joy at the same instant. The second man was the man whose face she'd wished to see, only not where she had longed to see it. The man doing the chasing was Fire Chief Stein and he looked as young and handsome as he had fifty years before when he'd rescued her from the burning building. He was in uniform chasing the man with the red can and gaining ground on him fast.

Almost without thinking, Betty stuck her foot out in front of the terrified man to trip him. But he was young and healthy and she was old and frail. Instead of tripping him, the collision spun Betty around, slamming her into the wall. Stunned, she slumped to her knees, clutching her chest and gasping for breath. She opened her eyes and shook her head, trying to shake out the cobwebs that had grown there in the last few seconds. She heard a roaring in her ears, and figured the blow she'd taken had scrambled the part of her old, used-up brain that controlled her hearing, or maybe even damaged something worse. Then she got her head focused enough to distinguish where the roaring sound was coming from. Down at the end of the long hall where the kitchen was located, the smoke was heavy and black. She realized it was the roaring of a fire she was hearing. She still hadn't heard a fire alarm. That seemed almost impossible with what she was seeing and hearing. Then the thought came to her that she may well be the only one who knew there was a fire. She looked around and saw a red fire alarm box on the wall a half-dozen feet away on the other side of the hall. Recalling how frightened and helpless she had felt when the apartment building she'd lived in was going up in flames, so long ago. Miss Betty fought her way to her knees, holding on to the door frame of her room, and struggled to her feet. Shaking her head and trying vainly to spit the taste of burning from her mouth, she pushed her body off the wall and stumbled across the hall. She hit the far wall next to the alarm box, and with the last ounce of her strength grabbed the handle and pulled it down. Instantly, a dozen more emergency lights flashed on and a siren began screaming.

For a moment, she hung with the total of her hundred-and eight-pounds dangling from the alarm box, and her arthritic fingers feeling as though they were about to shatter like glass. Then her strength failed and she slid to the floor. But before she passed out, she heard the pounding of many feet coming down the hallway. She whispered, "It's about time." then before she blacked out, looked up into the eyes of the uniformed figure standing over her. He felt her wrist, and smiling, said, "You'll be all right, I promise."

The screaming siren the two Chiefs had heard as Dunn drove at the green Taurus like a torpedo aimed at a ship was the result of Miss Betty's heroic effort in reaching and pulling the alarm. After viewing the burned body at the foot of the steps, Dunn and Smythe-Bates climbed the steps and entered the building. The air was smoke-filled, but with the bright security lights they could see almost as far as the kitchen. Before they'd taken a dozen steps in that direction, Leonard Dunn yelled: "Christ no!" and started running. Smythe-Bates was right behind him. He found Dunn bent over Betty Peacemaker who was lying very still on the shiny tile floor, looking very small and lifeless. Dunn reached out and pressed his fingertips to her neck. Smythe-Bates asked: "Is she?" Leonard shook his head. "No, she's alive. But we've got to get her some help, Right now!" Smythe-Bates said, "I'll take care of her. You take care of that." He pointed down the hall at the black smoke pouring out of the kitchen. Dunn took a last look down at Miss Betty and said, "I love her." Smythe-Bates answered: "I know you do. I'll take care of her, I promise."

"Okay," Dunn's voice hitched. He stood and ran toward the kitchen.

At the end of the hall, past the kitchen door the emergency exit door stood open. He began to walk toward it and his feet caught in something heavy but flexible. Remembering the figure they'd seen burst out through the emergency door, he looked down, expecting to see a body lying there. What he saw surprised him nearly as much as would a body. At least a body would make some sense. Whoever the burnt man at the bottom of the steps was, he may have had an accomplice. Stepping over the object, he went to the kitchen door and looked inside. He saw that the fire suppression system had extinguished the fire, and the smoke was rising from smoldering equipment and other items, he backed out, leaving the door open to allow the smoke to escape. Then he hurried back toward Miss Betty. As he got closer, he heard her cough and then he saw she was sitting up. She looked up at him, smiled and said: "Hi Leonard: fancy meeting you here."

Dunn said, "Don't worry Miss Betty, you'll be okay!" She produced a huge smile: "I know, he promised. My head hurts a little, but our new police chief gave me CPR and did a fine job of it, too. Although I must admit that when I opened my eyes, I expected to see Chief Stein. I suppose he had to leave after he took care of business."

"Here we go again!" a male voice mumbled nearby. The two Chiefs looked up, surprised by the voice. The psychiatrist, Doctor French stood there shaking his head. Leonard Dunn was having none of it. He said: "You evidently haven't been knocked down yet today." French looked at Smythe-Bates and growled: "You're going to let him get away with threatening to knock me down and do nothing?" The Chief grinned and said: "No, I will definitely do something. I will hold you down while he beats you." Doctor Hamilton appeared from around the corner: "Let's get Miss Betty back in her room and taken care of before a championship Rugby match breaks out here in the hall. Then she looked at French and said: "I wish you'd go away before one or both of these men kick your ass, but only because I don't want to have to patch you up." Then she went into Betty's room and contacted the nurse's station for assistance. Sandi VanMetre was there almost immediately. Together they got Miss Betty into bed and hooked up to the monitors. Betty said: "I wish you wouldn't hook me up to that gadget, getting those patches unstuck from my chest is a bitch."

"If you wouldn't get into mischief and end up on the floor, I wouldn't have to do this," Doctor Hamilton replied, smiling. Betty blew her a kiss: "I'm fine."

"That bruise on your temple says differently. You may feel fine, but I want to be sure. What were you doing in the hall, anyway? And how did you get knocked down?" Betty said, "Pull up a couple chairs. I've got a story to tell you. And ask our two Chiefs to come in please."

Doctor Hamilton and Sandi VanMetre pulled the visitor's chairs up close. Chief Smythe-Bates stood at the foot of the bed. At Miss Betty's direction, Leonard Dunn sat on the edge of her bed. She took his hand and told them everything that had transpired after she woke up smelling smoke. When she finished, she asked them: "So tell me, am I crazy?" Dunn said: "Miss Betty, I believe every word. You're definitely worth coming back from the dead to save." His eyes were brimming with tears. She answered, "Well he's saved me four times now and this time he saved a lot of other people. Now he's not just my hero, I have to share him." She snickered as she said it. Dunn said: "I'd say you're quite a hero, you set off the alarm". Betty said "Do you think that will be enough to keep that jerk of a shrink off my case?" Doctor Hamilton said, "You don't worry about him. You just lie still and rest. "Yes doctor. I'll be a good girl." Then she got very serious, "I'm *not* crazy, am I?" Dr. Hamilton looked her in the eyes: "Not a chance in hell! Now you be quiet and try to rest. I'll send you in something for pain. Okay?" Betty tried once more: "Okay. Can I have a Bud Light to take the pain pill with?" Sandi hugged her and said, "If I could give you one without hurting you, I would. Now rest. I mean it!" Betty said, "Damn!"

"What?" asked Sandi. "I missed Jeopardy." Sandi was comforting: "Don't worry Miss Betty, tomorrow's another day." Betty had the last word. "I hope so. When you're my age, you don't assume anything." Sandi turned on her way out. "You take the pain meds Doctor Hamilton sends in. It won't be long until bedtime. Once you're properly relaxed, you'll sleep the sleep of the just. My shift's over. I'll see you in the morning."

CHAPTER 13

Proof Positive

As they walked to Chief Dunn's SUV, the two Chiefs talked about the destroyed Taurus that sat twenty feet away from the big vehicle that had slammed into it. And the fortunate fact that the fire hadn't spread farther. They talked about the fact nobody, other than Miss Betty, was injured. And Dunn said through a choked-up voice and a stream of sniffles: "Thank God she's alive! "Thank God," he repeated. When they passed the still-unidentified body at the foot of the concrete steps, Smythe-Bates said: "I'd give one month's salary to know who that is."

"Remember, I'm on the city council. I know a month of your pay isn't that much." Dunn's attempt at humor fell flat. Smythe-Bates said: "The town's paid plenty so far and I have not fully succeeded in doing what I was hired to do."

Neither of the Chiefs wanted to be the one to bring up the subject that was on both of their minds: Miss Betty's hero, Fire Chief Stein, and her insistence that he'd appeared once again to save her. When they got to the SUV, they saw the grill and bumper were a crumpled mess from the collision with the old Ford. Smythe-Bates asked: "Do you think it will still run?" Dunn shrugged. "Probably, but look at the damage, Eddie."

"I don't know. The forest green paint on the red looks lovely, sort of Christmas-like." Despite everything, Dunn laughed it off. Then he asked his new Police Chief friend. "What now?"

"Lenny, drop me at the police station so I can get my car, then I'm going home to get some rest and you should do the same. In the morning, I'll have the security company send me whatever all those cameras caught. Hopefully, it'll clear things up. We'll simply go from there. This entire mess is like nothing I've ever seen."

"Okay, let me know if you see anything that helps." Dunn said, and they climbed in the banged-up vehicle.

The next morning, the Police Chief called the Fire Chief and said: "Lenny, I've just reviewed the security video, you simply must see it!" Lenny stuttered, "Uh, Wh wh… why?"

"Words won't do it justice; you have to see this to believe it."

"Meet me at Care-Haven-Acres at nine when visiting hours begin. I'll bring my laptop computer. Miss Betty should see this, along with a couple of the staff members." The two Chiefs met in the nursing home's parking lot. Smythe-Bates said: "I want Sandi VanMetre and both of the doctors to be in Miss Betty's room when I show her the security video. If Doctor Hamilton thinks Miss Betty is up to it, that is."

"Dunn was skeptical. "You sure that asshole shrink should be there?"

"Yes, especially him!" The Police Chief insisted. "Go see Sandi first and ask her to get the doctors there ASAP." The police chief looked at his watch "It's show-time!" They entered the home and the Fire Chief went to the nurse's station to talk to Sandi VanMetre. The Police Chief walked in the direction of room 108.

Ten minutes later, the Chiefs were sitting in the visitor's chairs on either side of Miss Betty's bed. Sandi VanMetre rapped on the door. When Betty said, "Come in," an orderly carrying two folding chairs preceded Sandi into the room. Sandi told him, "Just leave them, we'll put them where they're needed." Sandi said, "The doctors are coming. But are you sure you want French to be here? He's not one of Miss Betty's favorite people." Betty spoke up: "You're right, I can't stand him. But if our town's police and fire chiefs want him here, make sure the ass wipe shows up." A knock came at the door. Dunn opened it and the doctors came in, French looking very uneasy. He gave the fire chief a frightened look. Then he said: "You wanted me here?" Leonard Dunn said: "Nobody wants you here, but the Police Chief says you should be here, so shut up and plant your ass in a chair." French gave Smythe-Bates a panicky glance. Smythe-Bates pointed at a chair. French sat down nervously.

The Police Chief had already set his laptop computer on the top of a chest-of- drawers where everyone could see it. He said: "Before I play this, I want to explain something. The security company took the individual images from the cameras lining the hall out there." He said, pointing at the door. "The cameras are motion-activated. Their computer program put them in sequence based on time-stamps and merged them into a video file. It works a little like a child's flip book. The images change so fast, it's much like watching a movie." He pressed a key and the screen came to life. The image was remarkably clear, considering the fact that the air in the hall was fouled by smoke. Movement was obvious, but initially hard to follow. Then as the image shifted to the next camera down the hall two figures became visible.

Smythe-Bates said: "You see two figures. As they move down the hall, the picture becomes progressively clearer. Probably because each camera in line is farther from the kitchen where the smoke was thickest. Start paying close attention now, this is where it gets interesting.

On the screen, the image clearly became one figure chasing another. Smythe-Bates explained: "If you'll notice, the first man is carrying what appears to be a petrol, uh pardon me, gasoline can. As Miss Betty had realized, the sheer look of terror was all over the face of the first figure. The farther the series of images progressed, the more obvious it became that the figure doing the chasing was gaining fast. It didn't take long for the two figures to get close to the emergency exit door.

Smythe-Bates said: "Watch this. I have viewed it a dozen times and I still can't believe it!" As the men got closer to the emergency exit door, the second figure disappeared. "Keep watching!" the Chief said. "It'll happen" "What?" asked Dunn but before the Police Chief could answer him, the image had changed completely. In rapid sequence, too fast for the eye to follow, the second figure was now in front of the man with the gas can.

Dunn was spell bound: "When did he pass him? I missed it." Smythe-Bates said: "You didn't miss it. He did not pass him.

He was behind him and then, just like that!" Smythe-Bates snapped his fingers. "He was in front of him. The time stamp on the picture proves that it happened in less than two seconds. Keep watching, it really gets hard to believe." Sandi VanMetre said: "It can't get any harder to believe." "Just watch."

Near the end of the hall, as the two running figures approached the emergency door, the lead man's head snapped back and he stood straight up, fighting to keep his feet under him. He was pin-wheeling the arm and hand that wasn't holding the can, desperately trying to keep his balance. The people watching the screen saw that he was still moving toward the door, stumbling forward with the impetus of his running charge. His momentum drove him toward the door, his feet unable to get a grip on the polished tile floor. Unable to stop, he slammed into the door. The bar across the door that said "Emergency exit only/ Alarm will sound" slammed forward, and the door flew open. At that moment he glanced upward and one of the cameras caught a full, clear view of his shocked face. Then he plummeted out the door, and out of sight. "Keep watching," the police chief said. "Here, they switched over to the view from the outside security camera." On the screen, the man stumbled out the door, and crashed down the steps, colliding with the concrete sidewalk. There was a huge burst of flames where he landed. The man twitched once, then again, and then he was still. Dunn whistled and said, "What in the hell happened?" Smythe-Bates said: "You'll want to study it yourself, but as far as I can tell when he fell, the can he was carrying split open when he it hit the concrete. Either that or the lid wasn't properly secured.

Either way, he became drenched with gasoline. The can must have thrown a spark when the metal hit the concrete. So, our arsonist went up like a Roman candle." Everyone in the room sat dumbfounded, literally unable to speak. Smythe-Bates went to the computer and pressed a couple keys. The video ran backwards till it reached the instant where the running man's face was perfectly clear. He stopped the video and said: "That's Raymond Bruce. He's a known fire-starter so seeing him wasn't a big surprise. This was!" He tapped a key and the video started backing up again. The Chief said, "It might take a couple tries to get this right." When he got the video where he wanted it, he pushed play. They saw the instant when the terrified man's head snapped back as though he'd taken a powerful uppercut to the chin. The Chief then paused the video and said, "Look close and you can see what caused him to go out of control and begin falling forward instead of running." Leonard Dunn walked to the computer and stared at the screen for a moment. Then he said: "I don't believe it. That's impossible. The brass-tipped fire hose had been pulled from its storage box in the wall and stretched across the hall. It appeared to be just hanging in the air, as straight as a Joe Montana pass. Then the fleeing arsonist reached it, and it caught him right across the throat. Dunn said, "That's what stood him up. It was like being clotheslined on a football field." Smythe-Bates smiled and nodded. "I know that whoever pulled the hose out knew how to open the hatch. And you said only firefighters are privy to that information."

"But what kept the hose taut? It was like somebody pulled on the nozzle end of it to set a trap." Smythe-Bates said: "Okay, watch closely. I watched this at least eight times overnight, and still can't believe it. He tapped the keys and the image was magnified. Everything became easier to distinguish. "Sandi VanMetre cried out: "Oh my God! There's a man standing against the other wall holding the end of the hose, keeping it tight. Who is that?"

The Police Chief said: "Look at his face and remember it. I'm going to show you something else. He fingered the keys and a still image appeared. It was the front page of The Martin's Grove Gazette.

He said: "That's the front page of the Gazette on March 26th 1972: the day after Betty Peacemaker was rescued from her burning apartment. Check out the picture." He enlarged it more and they could see a handsome man in a uniform. He had the face of the man holding the hose stretched across the hall. The Chief said: "I found this on the internet. Please read the caption." Beneath the picture it said: A photo of Fire Chief Philip Stein, who last night rescued Betty Peacemaker from the top floor of a burning building on Main Street. Everybody in the room was stunned into silence for a long moment. Then Leonard Dunn glared at Doctor French and yelled: "Alzheimer's my ass!"

Sandi VanMetre spoke up," Miss Betty, do you recall telling me to get over my George Baily syndrome and stop feeling sorry for myself?" Betty smiled and nodded. "Well", Sandi continued, "If I remember it right, the message George Baily received was that a person's life touches many other lives. When your guardian angel, Chief Stein, saved you, it meant you were there to touch God knows how many others." Smythe-Bates said. "Like all the students you kept straight." Dunn said: "Yep, there's no telling what some of them went on to accomplish or how many they helped. And there's no way I'd have become a firefighter without your story about your hero."

"Without Lenny's help, I'd never have figured out who we were chasing" the police chief added. Dunn said, "At least we know he won't be setting any more fires. I wish I knew why he was doing it. Do you think he was delusional and felt he was doing something good, like putting the residents of the homes out of their misery?" "I'm glad you asked that question Lenny. When I got to my car this morning, there was an envelope tucked under one of the windscreen wipers. Officer Johnson left it there during the night." Miss Betty asked, "What was in the envelope Chief?" "Johnson went back to Raymond Bruce's trailer for a more thorough search. In a box under the kitchen sink, he found Bruce's motive."

CHAPTER 14

Motive

The Chief opened a sheet of paper and read it aloud. The search cleared up several things. First, Bruce was no angel of mercy. In fact, he was just the opposite. There was a detailed family tree which showed that Raymond Bruce was the great-grandson of a colonel in Hitler's SS during World War two. Bruce himself was a neo-Nazi. There was a copy of Mein Kampf. There were transcripts of several of Hitler's staff meetings. What Bruce had hidden amounted to his manifesto. The text of one of Hitler's staff meetings referred to Hitler's euthanasia plans. His plan to exterminate the mentally ill and handicapped, thus cleansing the "Aryan" race." Hitler also believed that the old and infirm were a burden to the Reich and also should be eliminated. Raymond Bruce thought he was fulfilling Adolf Hitler's plan. "But why here in Martins Grove New Mexico?" Sandi asked.

He happened to live in what he considered a target-rich environment. A town with five elder-care facilities full of what Hitler had called the old and infirm," Smythe-Bates answered. "He didn't even have to travel." He turned the paper over. "Miss Betty, you have no idea how much horror and suffering you and your spirit of a hero prevented.

Johnson brought everything back to the station. Along with the manifesto and book, there were two bus tickets: one from here to Galveston, Texas, and another open-ended one from Galveston to Chicago. There are hospitals in both cities that specialize in treating children with birth defects. Apparently after Raymond Bruce had exterminated the old and infirm in Martin's Grove, he intended to take his show on the road and start exterminating those he thought might eventually pass on their physical disabilities to a new generation of potential Nazis. Miss Betty said: "He got what he deserved, good riddance to bad rubbish." Doctor Hamilton said: "Very poetic, and very appropriate Miss Betty. Then she said: "Well Doctor French, do you still doubt Miss Betty when she talks about her hero?" French looked at his feet and mumbled: "It's very convincing, but I'll have to think on the subject." Dunn said "Take all the time you like, think about most anything you want to think about, but don't think of sending Miss Betty anywhere. That could prove to be hazardous to your health." Instead of protesting, Dr. French said, "Understood."

Epilogue

After hearing about, and seeing the proof of the events that transpired at Care-Haven-Acres, the owner had an epiphany and drastically altered his business model. The facility's policy of pricing its services so only the wealthy were able to afford them changed.

When he rebuilt the part of the building damaged by fire, he added more rooms that were less extravagantly appointed, and priced them at a much more affordable level.

Another step in his effort to be a more productive member of the community, he offered to accommodate the people who had been displaced when the town's other facilities were destroyed. They were charged nothing. The owner said they had been through enough turmoil and heartache. They were welcome to stay until the other homes were rebuilt or the residents could make other arrangements.

Also, a large courtyard was added in the area between the two branches of the L-shaped building. It featured a big flagstone patio and a beautiful flower garden.

Sadly, Betty Peacemaker succumbed to a heart attack six weeks after the potentially catastrophic events at Care-Haven-Acres. Her memorial service was presided over by the pastor who had performed the wedding ceremony for Miss Betty and her husband in Santa Fe at the start of their brief time together.

The ceremony drew the most mourners of any ceremony ever held at Lander's Funeral Home. Near the end of the service the pastor asked if anyone would like to say something about Miss Betty. If they were standing in a line, the series of people who memorialized her would have stretched more than a hundred feet. The last person to speak was Doctor French. He was brief, but sincere. He said: "I didn't know Miss Betty well, which is something I regret. She was a friend to many people, but unfortunately, I made it impossible for her to consider me a friend. I was unfair to the lady. She was plain-spoken, and most often right. The last thing she said to me was, "Alzheimer's my ass." She was right then too.

Sandi VanMetre was promoted to Administrator of the home and held the position for ten years before retiring. The well-dressed greeter became her assistant.

Edwin Smythe-Bates and his wife Katherine decided to remain in the United States. They had become accustomed to the unhurried life of a small-town police chief. The following summer they vacationed with Leonard Dunn and his wife. They visited the ghost-town where many television westerns were made, including episodes of The Rifleman. And they traveled to Dodge City, Kansas and visited the site of the real Long Branch Saloon, constructed in 1878.

The following summer, both couples visited London, where Leonard Dunn saw that British policemen do carry guns, and that most people there drink their beer cold.

THE END